Letters
From an Attic

Letters
From an Attic

Three packets of letters that might have been

found in a trunk in an old Victorian house.

Letters that could have been written by three

generations of women, related by blood,

circumstances and the times of their lives.

Dorst Publishing

ISBN: 0-9713711-7-2

Cover illustration by Laura Wilder
Cover art © 2005, Laura Wilder

Published by: Dorst Publishing
A Division of Elim Publishing

Elim Publishing
1679 Dalton Road
Lima, NY 14485

Dedicated to

Ruth Green Fox
for countless hours of genealogical research

Michelle Judge
for sharing many hours of cemetery hopping

Sarah

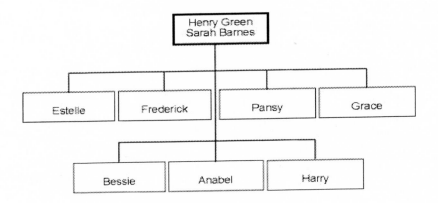

October, 1879

Dear Elizabeth,

Forgive me for being so lax in writing in recent months. I think the news I have to impart will explain the reason.

Do you remember the Green brothers over on West Lake Road? I think you met them at the Fuller barn raising summer before this past one. Mr. Henry Green and I have been walking out since June. Oh, Elizabeth, he is such a fine figure of a man! And he has a humorous way about him that is quite charming. I am sure you now have surmised what I am trying to tell you: we have set the date for our wedding, November 26th - his birthday! I am hoping you will do me the honor of standing up for me. Henry's brother, Charles, will be the best man. Please say you will! I have been busy sewing my trousseau. I found some nice brown faille (not too dear) for my wedding dress. I will add cream colored lace at the wrists and the dust ruffle will be of a cream taffeta. I also was able to get some flowered muslin for underthings and I will weave pink ribbon through those.

I do hope the weather will hold for the wedding and you will be able to come. We will be married in our parlor with the minister from the Presbyterian Church in town reading the service. The wedding is set for two in the afternoon to give everyone time to get here.

We will be living with Mr. and Mrs. Green to commence our married life, but I find it comforting that I will be just a piece down the road from my mother, in case my jelly won't "jell."

I hope you will remember our pact from long ago to stand up for each other when the time came for our weddings.

Your dear friend,

Sarah

January, 1881

Dear Elizabeth,

I am sending you news today of our firstborn child. Estelle was born on December 16. She is a beautiful baby (are all babies beautiful, or only to their parents?) and cries very little. The birthing was more than I had thought it would be but we managed to come through it. I am now up and about again and back to doing daily chores.

I do hope the election of Mr. James Garfield will prove beneficial. Cry shame that we women can not vote and bring our demands before the populace. I would surmise that some of Mr. Garfield's programs might aid the very poor of this country. The men will tell us women have no mind for the intellectual part of life. I, however, manage to read all of the local newspapers, not just the woman's page!

Henry and I have been attending several of the free concerts that are being held in the Public Square in Canandaigua. (The bandstand there was a gift from Mr. Frederick Thompson in the 1870s, and a very fine specimen it is.) It is exhilarating to hear the instruments playing in the open air. Many people come to listen and I am pleased to see they bring their children also. I am hoping that our children will have the benefit of a musical education, even if we have to be the ones to teach them.

Does Syracuse have any such public place where the people can gather for events such as this? I, as always, wish you had not had to move such a distance away. Who knows when we will meet again?

Love,

Sarah

April, 1882

My dearest Elizabeth,

I am so pleased to learn from your latest letter that you have been walking out with your church's vicar. I am sure he must be an extremely compassionate and intelligent man. Please be so kind as to tell me more about him.

I am keeping most busy currently. It is the time for spring housecleaning so Mrs. Green and I are attacking all the "bad" places with great vigor. We must take all the beds apart and wash each with a combination of Borax, alum and water to kill the insects. Of course, all walls, windows, pictures and floors must be done also. Then we beat every carpet in the whole house!

I do get more weary these days with the baby almost due.

We have some news. Henry has been hired on as a bookkeeper in one of the businesses in town. My Henry was not cut out to be a farmer! Charlie is the one brother who really works hard on the land and makes a good job of it. At the new occupation Henry will earn more money and perhaps we will be able to move to our own house sooner than we planned.

Your dear friend,

Sarah

August, 1883

My dear Elizabeth,

I hope this letter finds you well and enjoying your married life. You must be so busy with all the calls to make and your other duties as a minister's wife. Do write and tell me what it is like to live in a town and have social obligations.

Our third baby, Hattie, was born on June eighth. Stella, now not quite three, seems to want to be a little mother to the baby. Fred, of course, is still a baby himself at a little over one year. Henry is calling the baby "Pansy," and Stella has decided that is her proper name. The baby seems to have the colic and cries night and day. I have to make many milk sops to keep her quiet.

We will be moving into our own house soon. It is one that has not been used for some time so there is much in the way of outfitting it that has to be done. I spend a deal of my time now scrubbing down the walls and pine floors. I will be taking the wagon into town soon to search for calico for window curtains. Perhaps I can make a dress for Stella from the same material.

I look forward to being by ourselves. I have learned much from Mother Green during the time we have been here. She is an excellent plain cook and has a light hand with her pastry. But with William and Frank still living home, and our three little ones, it has been a bit crowded.

I had best close now and tend to my chores.

Love from your friend,

Sarah

June, 1884

Dear Elizabeth,

I am writing a very short note in with the two recipes you asked me to send.

In the Ontario Messenger is the news that Henry C. Work has died. Remember those old songs we used to sing around our piano: "The Grandfather Clock," "Father Dear Father, Come Home With Me Now," and "Marching Through Georgia"? He composed those, but the article also reminded us that he spent all of last summer in Canandaigua!

Pocketbook Biscuits

At night, mix together 1 pint of scalded milk, 1 teaspoonful of salt, 1 tablespoonful of sugar, 2 tablespoonfuls of butter, 1/2 yeast cake, and enough flour to make a soft dough. After kneading this thoroughly, cover, and place where it will rise. Early in the morning, roll out thin, cut into strips four by nine inches, one end square, the other pointed, fold each strip in three, the pointed end on top, fasten with a drop of water, and press a raisin into each point for a clasp. Bake like rolls.

Bertha's Popovers

Put the muffin tins in the oven to get very hot while you mix the popovers. Use 2 eggs, 2 cupfuls of milk, 2 cupfuls of flour, 1 scant teaspoonful of salt. Beat the eggs very light without separating. Pour the milk over them and beat again. Sift the salt and flour together and pour the eggs and milk into it and beat with a spoon quickly till all is foamy; strain through a wire sieve. Take the muffin tins from the oven, fill each one half full, and bake for twenty-five minutes.

I hope these will turn out well for you.

Love,

Sarah

March, 1885

My dear Elizabeth,

The new baby is another girl and I think Henry feels that we should somehow be able to even it out with a second boy. Gracie is proving to be an amiable baby, sleeping much of the time. Both Stella and Pansy are vying to be the one to take care of her.

We have heard the disturbing news that both typhoid and diphtheria are raging in the town of West Bloomfield. I trust these diseases will remain in the borders of that town and not venture into Canandaigua.

I found some pressed wood chairs for 94 cents each in the Sears, Roebuck catalogue. Now we can all sit down at the table together! It is starting to look quite homey now with more furniture and new curtains at the windows. The dry goods store in town had nice lawn material for which I gave 5 cents a yard, and it made up nicely into curtains.

Henry told me that, according to the Ontario Messenger, medical experts have predicted that former President Grant will not live five months due to cancer. That is very sad news indeed.

Your little Samuel must be ready to walk by now. Do write and tell me the things he is doing and how you arrange your duties as a pastor's wife with your motherly duties.

With love,

Sarah

November, 1885

Dear Elizabeth,

Sorrowful news to write today. Henry's little sister, Milly, was called beyond last week. She was but 16 years of age and had been taken with the pain of rheumatism much of her life. She was a very loving girl despite her infirmity and, of course, was much younger than her brothers. I do not believe you ever had the occasion to meet her when you lived here.

I have recently completed a new book by Mark Twain called "Huckleberry Finn." It is a most enjoyable story and told with a deal of humor. Are you familiar with his work? Many would think it is a book geared for children but I found it was also a treat for adults.

I have been thinking of late that I would like to try my hand at going back to teaching. You know I was doing that before Henry and I were married, and now I have more experience with children it might be a befitting occupation. Perhaps when the children are older I can consider this.

I have heard that some of the richer houses in the village are being set up with these new telephones. They have not run lines outside the village so I do not expect we will be having one for many a year. I confess I do not know how they can possibly work.

Hope all is well with you, Edmund and little Samuel.

Love,

Sarah

January, 1886

Dear Elizabeth,

This has been a very hard winter so far. We can barely keep the path to the barn open. We have put newspapers over the windows to keep the cold out, and the roads are so filled with snow they are only passable in a sleigh. I fear this will continue into spring, but there's nothing we can do to change it, and you know what we can't change we must abide.

To add to this problem the Chase's barn caught fire last week. (They are two places down the road from us.) The fire engine was not able to traverse the road so everyone was called out for a bucket brigade. I call to mind I thought the water would freeze in the buckets. I am glad to say the house was saved but the barn burned to the ground. Each of the neighbors is taking in some of the horses until another barn can be built. Lordy, things sometimes come in bunches.

I must close this short letter and get some chores done. It's almost too cold to sit and write!

Love,

Sarah

May, 1888

Dear Elizabeth,

I have just received your wonderful news! It is so nice that you now have a little girl. Is Sammy excited about the new baby? The best news of all, for me, is that you have named her Sarah. I consider that a great honor and am most pleased.

Our Bessie was born last month and so far is a good baby. All of the girls are very taken with her.

We are having a lovely spring and soon I will be getting to the spring cleaning that was delayed this year what with Bessie's arrival in the middle of what should be housecleaning.

Fred has just discovered roller skates which are very popular here. He spends all of his leisure time practicing. So far he has several scraped knees but nothing worse.

Henry has had an opportunity to get a better position. Mr. George Eastman has opened a camera business in Rochester and is in need of a chief bookkeeper. Henry has applied for the position and feels confident that he can succeed in getting the job. His brother, Frank, is also interested in working for Eastman in the department where they manufacture the cameras. These cameras are small boxes called Brownies and after you take all the pictures you send it to the company. They "develop" the pictures and return both the pictures and camera to you. If Henry and Frank obtain jobs there they will board during the week in Rochester and return home on the weekends. This will be difficult but the better pay will make a big difference.

Love,

Sarah

September, 1889

Dear Elizabeth,

I was so pleased to receive your letter in this last post. Thank you for the congratulations on Anabel's birth. She is our first blonde baby. Henry calls her Dennis. (I now know he really wants another boy in the family!)

The best news, of course, is that you are able to come for a visit. It will be such a pleasure to have time to sit and talk. One day while you are here I want us to visit the Canandaigua Hotel which is a very elegant place and has an excellent dining room. We can have their specialty which is lobster bisque. I think you will also be impressed by the decorations. It could be a hotel in a large city, I think.

Henry and Frank are both doing well at the Eastman company which is now called Eastman Kodak. (Mr. Eastman wanted a name for his camera company which would have a consonant at either end.)

I do hope that you, Edmund, Sammy and Sarah are all well. I have heard rumors that a serious influenza could affect this part of the country this winter. Perhaps we shall be lucky enough to avoid it.

I am finding it hard to wait patiently for your visit.

Love,

Sarah

September, 1892

Dear Elizabeth,

This has been a very difficult time. Bessie came down with Scarlet Fever three weeks ago. She was extremely ill and the doctor was very good about stopping in daily to see if there was any improvement. Someone had to sit with her day and night. It became difficult to think of anything but her illness. Thank goodness, she is now recovering - even her hair is starting to grow back.

Henry's brother, Charlie and his wife, Julia came to visit last week after the quarantine was lifted. Henry and Charlie had a nice chance to talk while Julia and I fixed dinner. They don't get to see each other often enough these days, with Henry being out of town during the week. The girls, Stella and Pansy, with questionable help from Grace (who is only seven), made tarts using the strawberry jam we put up this past June. They were declared a hit.

I am enclosing a photograph of us all. Henry had a photographer come out to take our picture for Harry's first birthday. This was an exciting event, but it does take a lot of sitting still and trying to look good!

I trust you are all well and the children are becoming more and more "grown-up."

Much love,

Sarah

October, 1895

Dear Elizabeth,

I grant you that having Henry working and living during the week in Rochester, has not been the easiest way to live, but we had fallen into a pattern that make it acceptable. Now my Husband, who has before now seemed to be a reasonable man, has decided on another change. I can write you frankly that this new idea is making me very uneasy.

He has heard that the New York Central Railroad is paying up to two dollars a day to men who work on the tracks and signals. He wants all of us to move to Tonawanda so he can obtain one of these jobs. I would prefer that we stay here, where all our families and friends are, and where the work he is doing has suited him very well. Needless to say, my opinion holds no weight.

Dear Elizabeth, please respond to this letter with the utmost speed and tell me what argument I may use to persuade Henry that this would be a foolhardy move.

Love,

Sarah

January, 1896

Dear Elizabeth,

We are now fully moved into our house. Fillmore Avenue is a residential area and it may be a little difficult getting used to living in a village. The houses are close together but the advantage is we are able to walk to most of the places we need to go. Fred is very pleased as there are sidewalks where he can continue to perfect his roller skating!

Gracie, Bess, Anabel and Harry have enrolled in school and will be starting classes next week. Even in a village there seem to be a number of skating ponds, even a river to skate on. I expect the young ones will continue to use our tea tray to coast down the stairway!

Stell and Pansy have both managed to find jobs as domestic help in two of the better houses. They should prove to be acceptable workers as they were always most capable around our house. Fred has been lucky enough to get a job as a delivery boy.

I do miss our home, all of our good neighbors and the families, but I shall try to make the best of our new situation.

I appreciate the advice you gave me regarding this move. You have certainly managed to adjust to your environment and are having a happy and full life. I shall try to be less selfish and get a better outlook on my new circumstances.

Love,

Sarah

February, 1897

My dear Elizabeth,

I find I am becoming more and more comfortable in Tonawanda. Anabel confided in me that she was glad we moved. Her chore, when we were in Canandaigua, was to feed the chickens. She said the chickens couldn't tell the difference between her toes and the corn. They pecked at both!

The neighbors here are very friendly and willing to help out when needed. We can exchange services. (I can help the newlywed wife who just moved in next door with her sewing and she can take Harry for me when I have to be elsewhere. She comes from a large family of younger brothers and sisters, so she has a way with children.)

The mention of sewing brings to mind the new Butterick Patterns. Have you found them available? The dress patterns are all printed on separate sheets of paper. This makes it easy to cut out a dress without having to prick apart an old one. I have in mind to make one for myself and one for each of the older girls.

Love,

Sarah

November, 1899

My dear Elizabeth,

Henry has given us all a wonderful surprise. He bought a piano! It is so nice to be able to have musical evenings again as you and I did when we were growing up. Stella, Pansy and Grace are all quite proficient at the piano and sheet music is readily available here, and at little cost. We already have these songs in sheet music: "While Strolling Through the Park One Day," "When You and I Were Young, Maggie," "Sidewalks of New York" and "Listen to the Mockingbird." We are having some great evenings around the piano. Both Harry and Anabel have nice singing voices. Harry's is especially beautiful and clear.

We have had some sad news from Canandaigua. Henry's brother Charlie and his wife Julia just lost their little girl, Anna Laura, at only three months of age. I feel so badly that we are not there to be of help to them at this sorrowful time.

I was pleased to read in your last letter that little Sarah is doing so well in school. She may grow up to be a teacher - like her namesake. How is Sam liking his new job?

Love,

Sarah

May, 1900

Dear Elizabeth,

I have not been able to write before now. Even picking up a pen is an effort almost beyond me. Nothing seems to matter. I can neither clean nor bake nor barely get up of a morning.

This is a tragedy that I had never thought would be my lot. Henry was killed in a terrible train accident on May 1st. I can not speak of the particulars as I dare not think of them. My mother is here so's to help and the neighbors have been most kind. The railroad people are doing their best to help us. I wrote them that I was left with seven children and little income. Henry's superior offered to let me borrow $25 until Henry's last pay check came through! They have also given Fred a job which is truly a godsend to us.

We buried Henry in the Tonawanda Village Cemetery and we are having a headstone made.

The neighbors have been bringing breads and desserts and roasts almost every day since the accident.

Please keep us in your prayers. We must hope that life goes on.

Love, even in sadness,

Sarah

August, 1900

Dear Elizabeth,

We continue to survive and this is mainly thanks to my children. Fred is handing over all of his earnings and the girls are also contributing. I guess it was a good thing Henry and I had so many children. Without their support and financial help I don't know where I would be. There is, of course, the emptiness in the house. No one now to holler: "Supper's on the table and Pa's half et!" No one to call Anabel "Dennis." And sometimes I think I hear Henry coming up the front steps.

But there is some good news also. Stella had met a Mr. Vielhauer, a business gentleman who seems to be a steady, hardworking man. (To my surprise he asked <u>me</u> for her hand, but I suppose I am both father and mother to the children now.) They had planned to be married this month with Pansh standing up for Stella. We then found out that Mr. Vielhauer was being transferred to Baltimone, so we had to hold the wedding despite being an unfortunate time but needs must..

We are well aware that it is against all propriety to have a wedding so close to a death in the family, but we kept the wedding small, and had it at home, so perhaps no one will decry us.

It is hard to think that Stella is so far from home, but she is an independent, confident young woman so I rest assured that she will do well.

I appreciate all the support that you and Edmund and the children are giving us also. Where would we be in this world if it weren't for good friends?

Love,

Sarah

April, 1901

Dear Elizabeth,

Such life affirming news I have! My first grandchild has been born. Estelle Annette Vielhauer was born March 22nd. Stella and her baby are doing well, the letter says. It is too bad they live in Baltimore which is so far from here, and I don't know when I will be able to see the baby, but it is exciting to be a grandmother!

I will be starting as a teacher in District #4 school in August. I am looking forward to this as I enjoyed teaching so much before Henry and I were married. I will be working with the older children and a teacher named Mary Ross will be teaching the infants. I am really so pleased that I got this job.

Pansy will be getting married in the fall. She is marrying a man named John Poss. He is a construction supervisor for the telephone company and will be working in Rochester after they are married. Pansy is hiring a seamstress to make her dress as sewing is not one of Pansy's talents. Grace will stand up for her and one of John's fellow workers will be his Best Man.

This year in the new century is holding so many new beginnings. May they all turn out successfully.

Love,

Sarah

May, 1904

Dear Elizabeth,

Another grandchild has arrived. Stella had a baby boy, Jack, and all are well. It is such a strange feeling knowing that these little ones will carry on the family. At the same time I received the very sad news that Charlie and Julia lost another little girl, Millie May, 6 months of age. My heart goes out to them, losing two children. It is times like these when I realize how fortunate we have been and then I feel guilty that I should be blessed and others are not.

We are about to have another wedding. Grace is marrying Harry Wheeler next month. He is a kind, handsome, quiet man and a talented designer for a lithograph company. (I had to ask, too: it is a company that makes the paper covers that go on canned goods and Harry does the attractive pictures on them.) They will be renting a house on Sidney Street, just a few blocks from Pansy and Jack's place.

School is about finished for the summer, so we are busy doing testing and making sure all the children have gotten what they needed out of the school year. I think at least two of the older students will be going on to secondary school and that makes me feel as if I have done my job well.

How does Sarah like school? I am so pleased she wants to be a teacher, too. Will she be going to Normal School in the fall?

Love,

Sarah

October, 1906

Dear Elizabeth,

I have delayed in writing as this has been a very difficult time for us. I now know, first hand, how dreadfully sad it is to lose a little one. Stella's Alice died in an unfortunate accident. Little Annette, who thought she was being helpful, picked up the crying baby from her buggy and dropped her. They brought her body up here and we buried her in Henry's grave. I think it pleased Stella that we did this.

It isn't often they can make the trip up here from Baltimore, and I was glad to see all of them, despite the unhappy reason for their coming.

We decided, since Stella gets here so seldom, to have a formal picture taken of the family and I have enclosed one for you. It is still amazing to me how the process works but I thought the picture turned out very well.

The newspapers are full of stories about the terrible earthquake in San Francisco, California. So very many died and so many more were injured. I can think of nothing more upsetting than to have solid ground beneath you just disappear. Can you imagine how hard it will be to rebuild all those buildings, as well as to start all over again with the businesses?

This is certainly not a cheerful letter and I am sorry to burden you with my problems.

Love,

Sarah

November, 1907

Dear Elizabeth,

We have had another wedding in the family. Bess married Bill Rohrdanz in June. Bill works for New York Telephone and Bill and Bess are renting a house on Ward Street in Geneseo. They are expecting their first baby in March. Bill is nine years older than Bessie so I think he was ready to start a family.

Anabel helped a lot with the wedding arrangements. She made Bessie's dress as well as her own, as she stood up for Bess. I was happy she was able to do this as I started having a few headaches around that time.

I have been feeling rather unwell with the headaches and also a weakness on my left side. I finally went to a doctor and he thinks I may have a brain tumor. I told him I don't have time to get sick. I still have my teaching job and three children at home. "This, too, shall pass," I said, and he said he hoped so.

Fred will be getting married also this coming January 29th. He is marrying Gertie Johnson and they will live in Buffalo. Fred is still with the railroad and doing well. He has been so good, helping with the household expenses since Henry died, and he has been like a father to the younger children. I am happy he will be having a family of his own.

I have been enjoying listening to Harry and Anabel singing after the supper dishes are done. "Just a Song at Twilight," "In the Evening By the Moonlight," and "I Wonder Who's Kissing Her Now," are some of my especial favorites. It's a nice way to close a day.

Love,

Sarah

March, 1908

Dear "Aunt" Elizabeth,

It is with great sadness that I write you to say that Mother died quietly on March 1st. We are all in mourning here and we mourn for you also in your loss of a lifelong friend. This last illness was a difficult one but she was brave throughout.

My sister, Bessie, is due this month with her first child. Mother overcame her own distress to carefully tell me how I will be able to help Bess when her time comes. She thought of her children first before herself despite her illness.

We will be burying her in the Tonawanda Village Cemetery, next to our father.

My sister, Grace, and her husband have generously offered to take Harry, as he is too young to be on his own. They live in Rochester and I am sure Harry will find this to his liking. (Grace is expecting her first child in October.)

We all send our condolences to you who have been such a dear friend to our mother. Please keep us in your prayers as we all go our separate ways.

Sincerely,

Anabel

Anabel

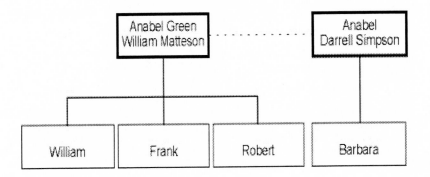

Anabel Green
William Matteson

Anabel
Darrell Simpson

William | Frank | Robert | Barbara

June, 1908

Dear Leah,

We are all sorting out our lives now that Mother is gone. I am going to try to find a job in Rochester. My sister, Grace, and her husband Harry, live there and they have taken my brother Harry to stay with them. (They are expecting their first baby in October and I feel this is a very kind move on their part.) Harry is only 16 so he is too young to be on his own. If I can get a place in Rochester I can also keep on eye on him.

My friend Mildred Taylor is working there now and she says she is pretty certain she can get me a job at the printing company she works for. Then we could live together in her boarding house also. I have my doubts that it will be as easy as it sounds, but I guess I will do whatever is necessary. I know one thing I will miss greatly in a boarding house and that is cooking, which I love to do.

I am sorry I can not be more cheerful. When I look squarely at my life that is coming up I am extremely fearful. It is like walking into a deep lake and not being able to swim.

Love,

Anabel

May, 1910

Dear Leah,

It has been some time since I have written but there has been a lot going on here.

Do you remember me telling you about Bill Matteson, the man I have been stepping out with? It has really become serious and we are talking about marriage. Bill has been working as a salesman and he has earned some bonuses from his sales. Enough, he thinks, so we can now plan on our future.

I have been looking at material to make a dress for the wedding. My sister, Grace, will stand up for me and Bill will have his good friend, Darrell Simpson, as Best Man. We will be married by the Reverend Beaven who is the minister at the church where we all sing in the choir.

We hope to be able to rent a house, or flat, in the Lake Avenue area which would be close to stores and a trolley line.

I hope you are enjoying your new job and your new town. I am sorry it is so far from here but perhaps sometime we can plan a trip out there to see you.

Love,

Anabel

October, 1911

Dear Leah,

Such good news in your last letter! I am so happy for you. Tell me more about your intended. Where does he work? Is his family in the area?

This brings to mind how much I am missing my family. When I was working I was too busy to notice but now it feels like there is a big hole in my life. My sister Grace does bring Bobby and comes to visit from time to time. (She says if I had a telephone she would call me daily, but, of course, I don't.) My oldest brother, Fred, is living in Buffalo with his wife Gertie, and my brother Harry is also in Buffalo now. (They both work for the New York Central Railroad.) My oldest sister, Stella, is in Baltimore and Pansy and Jack have purchased a house in Rochester, near Grace and Harry (in the Culver Road area.) Bessie and Butch are in Geneseo, and we keep in touch by letter. But I could wish a few of them were closer.

I guess it's a good thing we don't have a lot of furniture in our house. Billy is walking now (and climbing) so it could be even more of a problem with tables and chairs around!

The one piece of furniture we have that I wouldn't give up is our piano. The Rochester schools were putting new pianos in all of the schools so the old ones could be had for the taking. Sometimes of a Sunday evening Darrell comes for supper and the three of us have a musical evening. Darrell has a fine, clear tenor and we all blend well together.

Love,

Anabel

December, 1912

Dear Leah,

I don't think I will complain about not having much to do now. Our second boy, Frank, was born last month. And Billy is continually looking for new mischief to get into.

Bill is now a traveling salesman during the week. This has made our money even tighter than it was before, as rooms and meals cost more on the road. I am still making all of Billy's clothes but Frank will be able to wear his old dresses and other clothes for quite a while. I knitted so many soakers for Frank before he was born that they should suffice. I did find some good wool that was marked down in price so I am making Bill an overcoat for Christmas.

I am so glad to see in the newspaper that Woodrow Wilson has been elected President. He seems to be a competent and reasonable man. I hope he will be good for the country.

I still do not have one of those washing machines but now I have a hand wringer, which does make the wash easier to do. We have lines in the backyard so I can hang the wash out winter or summer.

I have just heard a F.W.Woolworth's Five and Ten Cent Store is opening downtown. I am very anxious to be able to go see it. It sounds as though it would be a very popular establishment! Do you have one in Detroit? I'm glad the trolley passes nearby so I can get downtown, although trying to take two babies along does not sound like it would be easy.

Best wishes for a Merry Christmas.

Love,

Anabel

August, 1914

Dear Leah,

The war in Europe is a terrible thing! So many countries are involved. I am just glad we're not in it.

I am expecting again in October. I hope this one will be a girl. Two boys are enough problem for anyone. It seems like every other year I have a baby, and the years between I lose one. It does keep me busy with all the cleaning, cooking, washing and taking care of the boys. And, speaking of children, Pansy and Jack adopted a baby, Kathryn, last year.

There is a new Chaplin movie at our neighborhood theater - "Tillie's Punctured Romance." Marie Dressler is in it also and I do enjoy watching both of them. I hope we will be able to see it when Bill is home this weekend.

My friend, Mildred, has now decided she will set her cap for a rich man. She says it is just as easy to fall for a rich man as a poor one. Also she says if you are going to be unhappy in a marriage money would help. We'll see if she proves right.

How is your new house? I am eager to hear all about it and how you will decorate it. Grace sometimes gives me her old copies of Delineator Magazines and I love looking at the rooms in them.

Love,

Anabel

May, 1917

Dear Leah,

I meant to write you earlier about this but all the war news put it out of my mind. My youngest brother Harry married Maud in Buffalo in December. I would like to have gone to the wedding but we couldn't drive since we don't have a car, and Rochester and Buffalo being famous for their snowstorms we didn't want to take a chance on the train.

Now we too are in the war "over there," and I just hope we will be able to bring it to an early end. Darrell has been inducted and is shipping out soon. Since he has been placed in Intelligence, he thinks he will be stationed in Paris. I am sure we will feel the effects of the war here even if we aren't being attacked. I am already noticing a shortage of sugar and they say that other foods and fuel will be curtailed, too. Also, I am putting down eggs in waterglass, for baking. Is your husband going to have to serve?

The boys are growing fast. Billy is a very smart, curious boy, always wanting to know how things work. Frank, although he looks angelic, loves sports and wants to play baseball like his dad and his "Uncle" Darrell. Bob is given to throwing tantrums if he doesn't get his way!

I wrote you about Mildred's marriage to O.B. last year, didn't I? She certainly found her rich man and they have a beautiful house, and she has all the furs and jewelry she could want. They have just had a daughter, Margaret Alice. I made Mildred what I make all new mothers - a mosquito netting for the buggy. Plus I knitted a jacket and bonnet. Nice to make something in pink for a change!

I hear that women here and in England are "bobbing" their hair. I don't think I will cut mine. I mostly wear it up in braids wrapped around my head, so it is out of the way. I believe the hair cutting is a part of the women's suffrage movement. This may be something that will happen in years to come but I don't think it will happen soon.

Love,

Anabel

November, 1918

Dear Leah,

It is such a terrible event I can hardly bear to write it. I find it hard it believe it actually happened.

Two weeks ago I was working in the voting booth when I was surprised to see Bill, who was working out-of-town, come in. He looked awful. His eyes were sunken and glazed, he was flushed and he had dark spots on his face.

He said he had a bad cold and came home. I told him to go home and go right to bed and I would be there as soon as I could. I went to a nearby store and called Grace. I told her what happened and asked if she could go to my neighbor's to pick up the boys and take them home with her. I called the doctor and asked him to see Bill. He said he was already overworked with people with this flu and there were no nurses available to send. We were both fearful that Bill had what is being called the Spanish Flu. I went home as fast as I could and started putting cold cloths on Bill's forehead and cleaning up after he was sick. By this time he was delirious and just tossed and turned. This went on through the night and late the next day he died.

There have been so many people here all ill with this flu. They say many in the military are also dying of it.

I arranged a small funeral for Bill. (They could not bury him as there were so many before him still waiting for burial.) I came home alone from the service to bake a cake for Bob's fourth birthday.

I have no idea what will happen to us. We, of course, had no money put aside for an emergency. I will write more soon.

Love,

Anabel

November 11, 1918

Dear Leah,

Armistice Day! There is a great deal of excitement here and I suppose it is like that everywhere in this country. This is the day we have all been waiting for! Now we can get back to our everyday lives and not have to worry about all the poor soldiers.

I have heard from Darrell since I wrote to him of Bill's death and he wrote to say when he returns home he will help out, as he is the godfather to all three of the boys. That was a very kind thing to say, I thought.

I went to the printing company and out of desperation I almost <u>demanded</u> a job - and I got one! I will be starting next week. This is making me feel much more confident and it makes my outlook much brighter.

I think we will be able to stay in this house as the landlord is being very understanding and not insisting on more rent. (I think all the rents are being raised in the neighborhood so I am grateful mine is not.)

Frank and Bob have had so many sore throats lately that the doctor felt they should have their tonsils out. There is a new Dental Dispensary on Main Street where they do the operating and keep the children in overnight. I took the boys over last week to have it done. (This is a free service for those who can not pay.) When I picked them up the next day the doctor told me all went well except that Bob hemorrhaged during the night. They think he might be a "bleeder." On the way home Frank told me, "Bob kept crying but I told him it wasn't so bad. But he cried anyway." Bob seems fine now, thank goodness.

Love,

Anabel

May, 1919

Dear Leah

It has been difficult these last few months and I am sorry I have fallen down in my corresponding. Working and taking care of the boys and trying to keep up with the cleaning and washing and cooking, I fear I have little time for much else. Lord knows when I will get to the preserving this year!

We had a little incident that lightened our spirits somewhat last week. I always fix the boys' lunches before I go off to work in the morning. This particular day it was a slice of bread, some cheese and an oatmeal cookie each. I set it out on the kitchen table and they come home from school at noon to eat. On this day they came home and each plate was empty! When I came home from work that night the boys were pretty angry. (They had to scout around for something to eat!) It turns out that the little girl next door had wandered in our house and helped herself! I told the boys I thought we were the only family on the street with our own Goldilocks.

I received a very sweet letter from Darrell yesterday. He wrote he hopes I won't think him presumptuous but he has always loved me and would like to marry me as soon as the mourning period is over. He expects to be returned to this country in July and I can decide then. He also said that he has been godfather to the boys all this time and now he would like to be their father. Can you imagine such a thing? I am overwhelmed!

This is going to take some thinking about. I am very fond of him but it would be a big step anyway.

Love,

Anabel

November, 1919

Dear Leah,

Darrell and I were married on November 17th, in a small wedding. His friend Jim Bellis was Best Man, Mildred stood up for me, and the minister was Rev. Beaven, who had also married Bill and me. We left the boys with Grace and Harry and went on a weekend honeymoon to Toronto. What an interesting city that is!

Darrell is now the assistant manager at Westinghouse, and he says they are good people to work for, and he enjoys being there.

We have rented a house on Field Street and have gotten some nice pieces of furniture. Of course, we have the piano and it is such a good way to spend an evening singing "Pack Up Your Troubles in Your Old Kit Bag," "Roses of Picardy," or "There's a Long, Long Trail A-Winding."

It is strange that Darrell and Bill were good friends as they were complete opposites. Darrell enjoys being home of an evening, reading or sometimes we play the phonograph and dance. This makes the boys laugh as they think it's "mushy."

Before we got married we discussed the disciplining of the boys. Since I had been the one in charge of them before, we decided to continue that practice.

Billy still calls Darrell "Uncle Darrell" but both Frank and Bob now call him "Dad." That seems to please him a lot, as it does me.

I have written enough of my doings! Now you must respond and catch me up on what is happening where you are.

Love,

Anabel

October, 1920

Dear Leah,

We celebrated Bill's birthday week before last (he informed me that now that he is ten he is "Bill" not "Billy") and we gave him a chemistry set. He has always been one who wanted to know what made things work, and how they were put together. He has done several experiments since he got the set but the other day he set the dining room curtains on fire. Up until that time his experiments were mostly just bad smells. Now he has to confine them to the cellar.

The other day I took some soup over to a sick neighbor and when I came home I found a trail of what looked like blood leading all the way up to the bathroom. It seems Bob had tried to hitch a ride on the ice wagon, fell off and cut his chin. I guess he is still a bleeder. It does seem with boys there is always a crisis.

There are several young boys in this neighborhood so Frank keeps busy playing baseball (in the street) and has now decided he would like to learn to box. Bob has some friends, too, but their group is mostly cowboys and Indians.

I have to find a day this week to go to the stores for material for curtains to replace the dining room ones. I may even have to go downtown to find some. Our biggest department store, Sibley, Lindsay and Curr, usually has a fine selection of fabric.

Love,

Anabel

July, 1921

Dear Leah,

I just heard from my brother Fred that he and Gertie had a little girl last month. I'm sure, by now, you must have lost track of all my family so I will get you up-to-date:

Stella has Annette who is now 20, and Grace, 9. Jack died in a boating accident two years ago and Alice died as a baby.

Fred and Gertie lost their first boy, Fred, Jr., at 9 months. Kenneth is now 9, Gilbert is 8, Dawn is 3 and Shirley is the newborn.

Pansy and Jack have Kathryn who is 8.

Grace and Harry have Bob who will be 11 in October, and Betty who will be 2 in September.

Bessie and Butch have Bill, 13, Sherwood, 11, and Paul, 2.

We have Bill, 11, Frank, 9, and Bob, 7.

Harry and Maud have Ruth, almost one and one half years old. Their first baby, a girl whom they named Betty, only lived ten weeks. She had some kind of digestive problem and then got the flu. She died on September 16th, so when Harry and Grace's girl was born on that date they named her after this baby.

Thanks to Grace, who will use any excuse to have a party, we do get together as a family once a year. We have a picnic at Letchworth State Park. This is a beautiful place with gorges, waterfalls and nice treed areas for picnicking. We bring fried chicken, potato salad, macaroni salad, all kinds of homemade pickles, Grace's famous baked beans, lemonade and beer for the men, devilled eggs, and I always have to bring my mahogany cake.

It is a good chance to catch up on news and for the cousins to get to know one another. I think it is sad that many families lose touch with each other if they move out of their home towns. I am glad that you and I have kept up our friendship, even if it is only by letter now.

Love,

Anabel

January, 1924

Dear Leah,

I finally have my girl! I had the baby at home as there was an epidemic of impetigo in the nursery of the hospital. It turned out that the baby was a breech birth which accounted for the long, difficult labor. The boys were forced to stay on the front porch and a cold stay it was. Anyway, we are all pleased she is here, and Darrell is so proud. The doctor ordered a nurse to come in and this has been a great help. We named her Barbara Carolyn (the Carolyn after Darrell's mother) and she has lots of black hair, which I know will fall out. The boys all went around and told their friends they had a sister. Most of their friends (who already have one) weren't impressed.

I fixed up a small room next to the bathroom for the baby. I don't know what the other people who lived here used it for - it is too small to hold a bed or dresser - but it works well for a cradle.

I was so pleased to hear you have completed your nursing schooling and have found a job at one of the hospitals in Detroit. You said you were afraid you would be "so old" compared to the other nurses but I am sure they will appreciate your maturity. What ward will you be working on?

Love,

Anabel

March, 1926

Dear Leah,

241 Terrace Park - our new address! Our house is simply wonderful! Everything is so new, and clean! We have a kitchen (with a breakfast nook), a dining room and a living room on the first floor. The living room has a gas fireplace with built-in bookshelves on either side. Upstairs there are three bedrooms, a bathroom and a full attic. We also have a cellar with a cement floor, so I can hang the wash inside to dry if it is raining. And we have a garage.

There seem to be more farmers selling their goods than there were in the other places we lived. We have a milkman, a baker, a vegetable cart, sometimes a butcher comes around also, and, of course, an ice truck for the ice box.

We live only a few blocks away from South Park which is nice for the boys. They can go there to play baseball and they can swim in the river. There are two families with little girls Babs' age so she will have playmates.

Of course, there is no grass or large trees but all that will come in time. I would like to have a flower garden in the back yard if I can.

Bill and Frank are both going to the high school that is fairly close and Bob will go there next year. Frank is especially pleased with the school because it has a very fine art department.

I still can't believe we own our own house! "New houses bring new babies," as the saying goes, and I am due in August. It will be nice for Babs to have someone closer to her own age than her brothers.

I had been looking forward to making lots of pretty dresses for Babs but all she wants to wear are bloomers! So much for having a girl!

Love,

Anabel

September, 1928

Dear Leah,

This summer we are having exceptionally fine weather. Nice, warm days with lots of sun. How is your weather there?

One of the nicest things about living here is that we are much closer to Mildred and O.B. We go to their house, on Arnett Blvd., every Saturday night to play bridge. It is such a lovely place! She has Oriental rugs on the floors, a working fireplace in the living room, and a nice alcove for their piano. We always get a chance to have a conversation with Margaret Alice - the sweetest little girl. She has a charming smile, and she is always so pleasant to talk to. Despite all the things her parents have given her, she doesn't have a spoiled bone in her body.

Mildred has a very lovely circle of friends and they have included me in their doings. Once a month we get together for lunch at each other's houses and then play cards. We call ourselves "the girls" and my boys think that is the funniest thing they have heard. We are all in our late thirties!

Our piano gets a lot of use. I play, of course, only for my own pleasure, and Bob has been learning. He has three favorite songs that he plays over and over: "Bye, Bye Blues," "My Blue Heaven," and "Am I Blue?" Darrell knows several chords and from time to time sits down, plays them seriously, then gets up. Even Babs is starting to pick out tunes. Grace and Harry's kids - Bob and Betty - can play anything they hear once by ear! That is truly a talent!

Bill found out just before he was to graduate from high school that he failed Civics, so he couldn't graduate. I suggested he go to summer school, or take a P.G. course in the fall but he insists he is going to join the Navy. Maybe it will be good for him. Bill is not good at disciplining himself and perhaps the Navy will instill something in him that I haven't been able to.

Love,

Anabel

May, 1929

Dear Leah,

I'm sorry I haven't written lately. We have had a hard time here but I hope the worst is now over.

Babs was doing very well in kindergarten. The only thing she didn't like about it was snack time when they had milk, which she doesn't like. (We solved that by adding Ovaltine.) Shortly after her fifth birthday she came down with whooping cough. She had a very hard case of it and, instead of getting better, it got worse. We could only sit by her bed and read her stories. As soon as one story was finished, she would say, "Read." It was good the boys were here to spell Darrell and me. Now she is up but if we go outside we have to take her in her old baby buggy as she is too weak to walk. She has now been out of school this whole semester but the teacher said she will go into first grade in the fall.

We hear from Bill fairly infrequently, but he seems to be doing well in the Navy. He has been made a Pharmacist's Mate, which will serve him well when he looks for a job after he gets out. He is now stationed in Panama, and says the climate is wonderful. The sun shines almost every day and it is nice and hot.

Some good news, though - we now have a telephone and are on a four-party line. We made a small shelf for it that fits in the breakfast nook, and, yes, Grace does call me daily (as she had said she would many years ago), mostly to tell me what she did the day before and what they had for dinner.

Love,

Anabel

September, 1930

Dear Leah,

We had our first high school graduate this year. Frank graduated from West High School and won an art scholarship to Syracuse University. We were all so excited for him! After graduation he and a friend decided to spend the summer bumming around the country. They did make it as far as Chicago and it was a very enlightening experience for them both. He is looking forward to going away to school. He was always sketching things, and people and making cartoons, but now he can learn more about actual painting. I do hate to see him leave but he will no doubt be the better for it.

This has been an eventful time. As bonuses Darrell has been able to get a gas stove, a refrigerator and a radio at reduced prices. I can't begin to tell you what the stove and refrigerator have saved in time and mess. No more having to empty the icebox water (or, if forgetting it, wipe up the water), no more having to remember to put the sign in the window for the number of pounds needed! The gas stove cooks so well and is much easier than a wood stove. I will now cook everything I can think of!

This summer Babs and her friends put on a play in the neighbor's garage. I was chosen to make the costumes (out of crepe paper). They put on Goldilocks and it was fun for all.

Darrell recently pointed out a small article in the local paper he thought I might be interested in. Indeed I was. It said Kodak had added three additional stories to its building on State Street. I don't know if I ever told you or not, but my father was chief bookkeeper at Eastman Kodak Company for several years. With the addition of the new stories this makes Kodak the tallest building in Rochester.

Love,

Anabel

January, 1931

Dear Leah,

Darrell has lost his job, along with almost everyone else we know. We do have some savings but they will not last long trying to feed five of us. (It is good that Bill has his job at Strong Memorial Hospital, where he can live with the interns so that's one less person here.)

Frank has decided to get a job in the CCC - the Civilian Conservation Corps. They hire young men to dig ditches and do any kind of manual labor, or otherwise, that will benefit the community. They pay $30 a month and that should help to keep us going for a while.

I am sorry to say that I think Frank and his friends are starting to drink. I worry about what they are drinking and, of course, the fact that it is against the law. Frank's friends are not bad - they just like to have a good time. I don't want him spending what little money he has on something that is not good for him. Unfortunately, he is not at an age where I can make him do what I want. He's always been my pride and joy and I don't want to see him get into trouble.

I am trying to find ways to make meals more cheaply and yet still have them taste good. I guess we won't be having as many desserts now, and that is what I love making the most. I like to find new recipes and try them out on the family but Frank keeps saying, "No apple pie? What kind of dessert is this?"

At least someone likes my cooking. Harry Wheeler, every so often, calls and asks if I can make something - maybe a dessert, maybe a main dish - and then brings photographers over to take pictures of the food. Of course, it is inedible after they shine all those hot lamps on it, but I am glad to do it, and he always pays me a little something for my time. I never get to see the pictures (they do them for advertising brochures for the company he works for) but I'm sure they turn out well. And I can feel I am doing my small part toward increasing our income.

Love,

Anabel

December, 1932

Dear Leah,

We have been in a state of shock for the last couple of months. A tragedy beyond belief has affected all of us. Mildred and O.B.'s daughter, Margaret Alice, was killed in a very unusual accident in October. She was having a horseback riding lesson and the boy who took the group out on the trail was fairly inexperienced. The trail goes over a railroad track and when the group approached it they could hear a train in the distance. The young man told Margaret Alice and another girl to cross the track and wait on the other side for the rest of the group who would cross after the train had passed. They crossed, Margaret Alice's horse was frightened by the train noise apparently, backed onto the track and was hit by the train. She and the horse were both killed instantly.

A reporter from the local paper came to Mildred and O.B.'s house and asked for a picture of their daughter. They had not even been notified there had been an accident! Mildred called me and asked if Darrell could go to the morgue and identify her. It is so hard to understand how such a dreadful thing could happen to such a sweet girl! I feel as though I have lost one of my own children.

The service was very nice. Reverend Mattice read a poem about the spirit coming to life in a garden "just beyond the wall." Mildred has been so brave through it all. She is always saying, "Remember when Margaret Alice did this or said that?" Not like some who never speak of the dead after they are gone. This way she is keeping her daughter alive in all our hearts. She also keeps fresh flowers on the mantle next to Margaret Alice's picture.

Frank is still working for the CCC which keeps us eating. I hope the election of Franklin Delano Roosevelt will mean that something good will happen to the country. The song that is popular now, "Brother, Can You Spare a

Dime?" is all too real. I like the romantic ones better, like "Goodnight, Sweetheart." We have a phonograph record of Rudy Vallee singing that and it is so pretty.

The day before Christmas we had another scare. I had sent Babs and her friend, Jean, to the corner store for day-old bread to make stuffing. Shortly after, Jean's father came to the door and said that Babs had been hit by a car, and the ladies who were driving had taken her to the hospital. I told Frank to get on the telephone and call the hospitals to see which one they had taken her to. After a couple of calls he said St. Mary's had a little girl in emergency and Jean's dad said he would drive me there. He has a Model T Ford and it stalled at every corner. I think he was more nervous than I was. It turned out that Babs had many cuts and one whole side was scraped but they thought it wasn't serious. However, they wanted to keep her overnight to make sure she had no head problems. So we brought her home on December 26th and had our Christmas then. I think the thing that impressed her the most that Christmas was that she could wear socks in December! (Her one leg was bandaged so stockings would be hard to get on. Also, it was 70 degrees outside.)

I can only hope that 1933 will be a year without so much pain.

Love,

Anabel

February, 1933

Dear Leah,

Good news! Darrell has a job. Mildred's husband, O.B., has started up an oil supplier company and has hired Darrell on as a salesman. He will be going to gas stations and persuading the owners to carry the Kendall brand of products. The "plant," as Darrell calls it, is on Scottsville Road which is only a few blocks away, but his customers are scattered all over Rochester. He will have some traveling to do but it is mostly in town. He is so relieved that he has found something at last.

More and more I have been getting men coming to the door asking for handouts. I have given them what food I could spare but I have asked them to do a job for it. Frank says they are called Hobos and asked if I had seen any markings on the back door.

There was one, when I went to look, like this. According to Frank that means "Nice woman lives here." He said he learned about the Hobos and their signs when he and Ranny were hitchhiking that summer.

Babs and her friends spend a lot of time at the park now. At this point they are learning to ice skate at the new rink there. In the summer they go on the Merry-Go-Round or just ride their bikes along the river. We were able to find her a used bike that works quite well. She is doing great with her piano lessons and the teacher at school has suggested Babs get private lessons rather than with a group, as she thinks she is quite talented. We will have to wait awhile for that until we get caught up with our bills.

Bob was supposed to graduate this June but he is still having problems with English so it may not be until next year. I just hope he doesn't get kicked out of school first. The principal has called me in a few times when Bob was caught smoking on campus.

I have finally gone to the doctor with some women's complaints and he thinks I need an operation. This is not a good time to consider something along this line, but maybe there never is a good time.

Love,

Anabel

March, 1934

Dear Leah,

Last week we had one day that was the coldest ever recorded in Rochester. Thirty-four degrees <u>below</u> zero! Can you believe that? Our neighborhood kept the young ones home from school as they would never have been able to walk it. Thank Goodness, it didn't last more than one day. Our furnace did its best to keep the house comfortable but we all huddled around the registers to get all the possible warmth.

We will be having our first wedding soon. Bill has been dating Florence Barone, a nurse at Strong Memorial Hospital, where they both work, and they have set a June date for the ceremony. Florence seems like a very nice girl - levelheaded and kind. She comes from a fairly large family in Mount Morris. They will be married in a Catholic church in Rochester so that will be a new experience for us.

Bob is going to graduate this June and after he finishes he wants to look for a job as a salesman. I would like to see him in an office job, using his math ability, but he wants to work with people. Speaking of jobs, Frank has found one as a bellhop at the Hotel Seneca. He should be good at that judging by how easily he makes friends with people, even strangers.

We just found out that Babs has been awarded a scholarship in the Preparatory Department of the Eastman School of Music. She will be taking piano and theory. This is very exciting. We could never have afforded their prices for lessons. This past year she has taken private lessons from Clyde Morse, who has had a musical program on the radio for several years, but I think the Eastman School will be able to give her a better education.

Love,

Anabel

August, 1936

Dear Leah,

Just a short note this time. Babs (I forgot - we're supposed to call her "Barb" now) had been taking lessons at the Eastman School for a few months when her teacher, Miss McCann, called. She asked what kind of piano Barbara was practicing on. I told her we had the old upright we had had for years. She suggested that, if there was any way we could do it, we get her a new piano. We started saving then and there. After two years we finally had enough to buy a baby grand. We wanted it to be a surprise so we made arrangements to have it delivered while Barb was at Camp Onanda with Jean and Phyllis.

Barb was signed up for two weeks of camp and she hated it. Every day we would receive a letter saying how bad it was and begging us to come and get her. We wrote back that it was only for two weeks and she would get used to it.

Finally the day came to bring her home. She talked, nonstop, the whole way home from Canandaigua, telling all the awful things she thought about the camp. When we got home she walked into the house, still complaining. When she reached the living room there was complete silence. I have never actually seen anyone speechless before but she was. So we knew then that she was pleased beyond words. That made all the scrimping and saving worthwhile. She so seldom shows enthusiasm for anything that this was a real treat!

Love,

Anabel

June, 1937

Dear Leah,

For years Frank has been referring to our house as "The Madhouse on the Hill." I finally asked him why. He said it was because his friends were always coming over, day or night. It is true that none of Bob's friends drop in, nor did Bill's when he lived here. Most of the neighbors don't have kids this age living at home so I can't compare it to them. Every Sunday from six to eight of Frank's friends come over to play pool in the attic. When it's time for supper they come downstairs to eat - all except Dave and Red Lamb, (their mother told them not to eat supper here; it wasn't fair to me.) So I send Barbara upstairs with sandwiches. Most mornings I'm not sure if we will have guests for breakfast or not. With the bed in the attic the boys all know they can sleep here if it's too late to go home. Often Johnny Atterbury will appear around nine in the morning, eat breakfast, then sit and chat for an hour or so. Bill Farrell comes over in the evening just to talk, whether Frank is home or not. I guess Frank's right - it could be a madhouse but I am pleased they all feel comfortable enough to do this.

Barbara graduated from Number 37 School last week. She will be going to West High School in the fall and is looking forward to it. I made her graduation dress out of some very pretty flowered lawn. The whole dress only cost 86 cents - including the pattern!! Many of the mothers at the school party said how attractive it was, and even Barb liked it! (Mostly she wishes she could buy store-bought clothes like the other girls.)

Love,

Anabel

July, 1938

Dear Leah,

Bob got a job at Land O'Lakes as a salesman and he has been living in Buffalo. He seems to be doing well. He doesn't write very often but a few months ago he did write to let us know he met a girl that he liked. Her name is Helen Berg and she is blonde with big brown eyes. She is a nurse, like Florence. Bob said they met at a play, sitting next to each other. I thought at the time the fact that he mentioned her at all might mean it was serious. And indeed it was.

Bob and Helen were married last month in a Presbyterian church in Buffalo. It was a very lovely, small wedding. Helen's parents were there and they seem like nice, down-to-earth people. It was an extremely hot day for June and when we got home and Frank asked how the wedding went Barb said, "It was so hot the rice we threw turned to rice pudding." It was an uncomfortable ride to Buffalo and back because of the heat, as you can imagine. Bob and Helen found an apartment on Delaware Avenue that is close to both their jobs, so they were pleased about that.

Frank is now working at General Motors in the factory. The pay is quite good and he is getting interested in joining the union.

Barbara is now very sad that her "best friend" since we have lived here has moved away. Jean Klein and her family moved to her Grandmother Hoffman's when her grandfather died. It's not too far away (they live near the high school) but it's a trip on a bike, and Barb doesn't like going alone.

And, of course, Jean is now going to a different grammar school. There is a group of friends that are in Barb's class that may fill the bill with Jean gone. One of them, Jean Swart, likes to read, like Barb, and has a great sense of humor. Hopefully, this will turn into a good friendship.

Barb tries to get all the newest popular songs, either in sheet music for the piano, or on records. Some of them seem quite odd to me, like "Jeepers Creepers," and "Flat Foot Floogie with the Floy Floy," but I do like "September Song" and "You Must Have Been a Beautiful Baby." Maybe I'm just old fashioned.

Love,

Anabel

September, 1938

Dear Leah,

Well, I am now a grandma!! Bill and Florence had a little girl last month, and she is darling! Her name is Barbara Jean and she has big eyes and dark hair which looks like it might be curly, like Bill's. They now live in Batavia (they both have jobs at St. Jerome's Hospital) so we won't get to see as much of the baby as we would like, but even a little is exciting. Barb, of course, is thrilled to be an aunt at 14 (none of her friends can top that), plus the big fact that the baby was named after her. There will be no living with her for a while.

Darrell and I have been going to the movies fairly regularly lately. It's nice to get out by ourselves with no children. We saw "Pygmalion" (I do love Leslie Howard) and "The Lady Vanishes." That last one is a really good mystery. We have three movie theaters near us: The West End, the Madison, and the Arnett. This makes it easy to see the movie we want and not have to go all the way downtown.

Both Barb and I have just finished reading "Mrs. Miniver," and enjoyed it a lot. I tried to talk Darrell into reading it but he said he will stick with his classics. He and his mother have both read all of Dickens, many times over!

Barb's piano teacher has been talking about her doing a solo concert in Kilbourn Hall. This is a concert hall attached to the Eastman School and Theater, where special students perform. The teacher wants her to do an all Chopin recital. It wouldn't take place until next year but Barb has already started working on it. We are so delighted with how well she is doing with the piano.

Barb seems to be fitting into high school well. She joined a sorority, she likes her English, French and art classes and loves chorus. Math is still her worst subject.

I hope to get some pictures of the baby soon and when I do I will send you one. I shouldn't say this, but she is one of the cutest babies I have ever seen.

Love,

Anabel

August, 1939

Dear Leah,

Harry and Maud have just announced Ruth's engagement to Jack Fox. They will be married next June. We haven't met him yet but Grace and Betty have and say he is really a nice boy. We are looking forward to the wedding.

There is a new family that has moved into Paul's old house (next to Klein's). They have one little boy who is about a year and a half. They have asked Barb to baby-sit him from time to time. The first time she went over was during the day. She had to get him up from his nap, change him, and feed him. I got several phone calls for information while she was sitting! But now she is more comfortable with him and he with her so it works out well. Several of Bob's friends have children also, so she is quite in demand as a sitter.

The other day she gave Darrell and me tickets to see "My Sister Eileen" when it comes to the Auditorium Theater. This is for our twentieth wedding anniversary which will be in November. What a nice present! We don't often get to see plays. Much baby-sitting money went into these tickets!

I guess Hollywood has decided this is the year for all the good pictures. We have seen "Goodbye Mr. Chips," "Made For Each Other," and "Midnight," with Claudette Colbert and Don Ameche. We want to see "The Wizard of Oz," which will be in color, and, of course, "Gone With The Wind." I loved the book, but I'm not sure about a movie four hours long - even with an intermission.

The world news is sounding quite disturbing. I hope there isn't another war brewing somewhere. Germany seems to want to take all of the countries around them, for whatever purpose. I'm not very political minded but these newspaper articles are upsetting.

All the young girls seem to be taken with a new singer, Frank Sinatra. Barb got the record "I'll Never Smile Again," and the girls play it over and over. I can't tell if it's the singer that is appealing to them or the sadness of the song!

Annette and Elmer had us over for a picnic last weekend. They are so good about entertaining! Barb suggested we take her bike with us as she isn't riding it anymore and she thought maybe Jean Eisele might like it. She was right. Jean was overjoyed. I'm glad she thought of it.

Love,

Anabel

July, 1940

Dear Leah,

We have just come back from Ruth's wedding to Jack. It was so pretty, and they even took a movie of all of us going into the church! The reception was lovely. Harry sang, "Because," "For You," and "If I Were the Only Boy in the World" in his wonderful voice. We had a great time and it was good to see the family again.

Darrell and I are sad because Barb has decided not to continue with her music lessons. She has been taking them for ten years and now she says she doesn't want to be a concert pianist nor a piano teacher which are about the choices she would have for earning a living at it. She feels she knows enough now to play for her own pleasure. We can understand but we did have hopes she would go into music. She continues to enjoy playing though and we still sing popular songs around the piano. Speaking of popular songs, the song "The Last Time I Saw Paris" reminds me that Frank's friends, Terry and Janet O'Connell, named their little girl Ellen Paris O'Connell. (A definite political comment.) Frank is going with a girl now that he seems quite fond of. Her name is Betty Slick but Frank calls her "Pretty." She's a nurse, too! What is it with my boys and nurses?

Bob and Helen are back in Rochester, living in an apartment over a dairy on Genesee Street. Bob is working for Ritter Dental and Helen is working at Genesee Hospital but is hoping to get specialing jobs soon.

We've seen some very well done movies in the last few months: The Grapes of Wrath (depressing but well acted), The Great Dictator (maybe if we can laugh at Hitler he will go away) and the imaginative Fantasia. All of them are worth seeing.

Love,

Anabel

August, 1941

Dear Leah,

I wasn't pleased at all when the government announced the peacetime military draft, but now Frank's friend, Johnny Atterbury, has been called up. Luckily, he will be doing what he does best - drawing for advertisements and other illustrations. He'll be stationed in California; still, it is taking him away from his family and his regular life.

Barb graduated from West High in June and she and Gini Hammon signed up for a summer course in Comptometry. The classes are held downtown and both girls seem to be doing very well. They will be finished the end of this month.

Mr. Klein said there is to be an opening in the Payroll Department at the Todd Company (where he works) and thinks maybe Barb will be able to get it. This is good news, indeed, as there are not a lot of jobs around for girls. The Todd Company is on University Avenue and, if she gets the job, the new bus line will take her directly there without having to transfer. It is such a blessing to have the buses now in place of the trolleys!

And now I have sad news to tell you. Bill has left Florence and Barbie. He said he was offered a good job out of town and Florence refused to leave, but I suspect this is just another one of his tales. I feel sorry for Florence but I do think she is better off without him. The worst part is that she is taking Barbie and going back home to Mount Morris. So we are being deprived, too. Life, sometimes, is too hard to think about.

Love,

Anabel

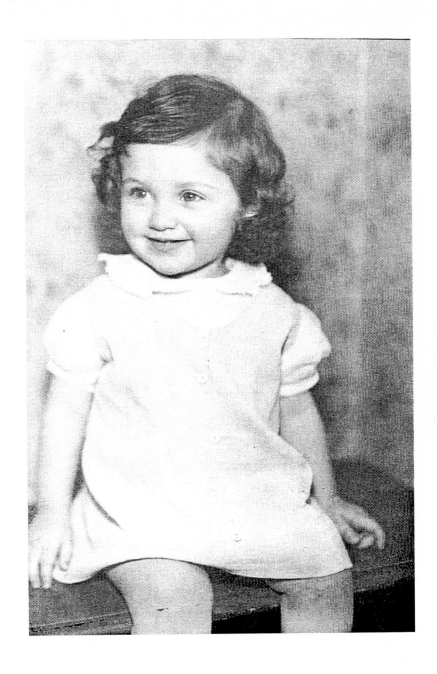

Barbara

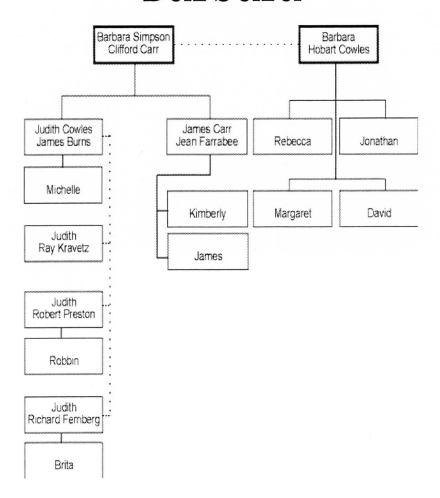

Barbara Simpson
Clifford Carr .... Barbara
Hobart Cowles

Judith Cowles
James Burns

James Carr
Jean Farrabee

Rebecca

Jonathan

Michelle

Kimberly

Margaret

David

Judith
Ray Kravetz

James

Judith
Robert Preston

Robbin

Judith
Richard Fernberg

Brita

September, 1942

Dear Jean,

I hope you are settling in at Cazenovia. What is the college like? What courses are you taking? Do you like your roommate? Am I being too nosy? Not being a college girl myself, you will have to fill me in on all the particulars.

Rochester is a strange city these days with all the young guys going off to war. Frank, Bob and Bill have now enlisted and mom has a flag with three blue stars on it in the window! Frank is in basic training in Texas in a division of the army called Chemical Warfare (scary!); Bob is in the Sea-Bees (nickname for Construction Battalion). This is a part of the Navy that goes in first to build housing for the troops to come. Bill couldn't get into our Navy because of his bad heart but they took him in the Canadian Navy.

My job is going along pretty well. They work us long hours but that's O.K. There are four of us girls in the Payroll Department - Janie, Florence, Virginia and me. Then there is our boss, Miss Hedges. She sits in the back corner of the office like a fat spider, smoke curling up from a permanent cigarette in the corner of her mouth. She had a stroke a few years back so she can't always tell when the cigarette is burning her lip. But we can.

I have been dating a guy who works in the Machine Division at The Todd Company. He's one of the few young ones left around here and he's really cute even though he is 4-F due to an automobile accident. His name is Cliff Carr and he's from a family of eight kids, brought up in Horseheads (near Elmira). I will keep you posted on how this works out. He's a great dancer, a lot of fun and much more sophisticated than anyone I have ever dated. I think I might be falling for him.

Several of the West High School guys are already in the service - Johnny Aagen, Paul Schmidt, Bernie Felch, Dick Hurlburt, Ronnie Buchanan, to name a few. They all look so grown-up in their uniforms!

Gini Hammon and Bob Leary were married last month. The whole feeling now seems to be let's not wait for what might be because it might never be.

We're starting to feel some shortages here and one of them is cigarettes. They are sending all the "good ones" to the boys, and we are smoking things called Wings, and Avalons and others I have never heard of. Remember when we first started smoking, you and I - up in our attic, near the window so we wouldn't be caught, and got so dizzy we nearly fell out?

Write soon, mon ami. Miss you.

Love,

Barbara

December, 1942

Dear Jean,

I was so sorry you couldn't stand up for me at my wedding but I know Aunt Kiki's should come first. Hope hers went well.

Ours was quiet, but nice. We held it in the small chapel at Westminster Church and Mr. Mattice did the honors. I wore a short, soldier blue velvet dress, very simple, with a blue veiled hat and a small corsage. Bob's wife, Helen, stood up for me, in a dark red dress and hat. Cliff's brother, Matt, was Best Man. We had a small reception at the house but I was so nervous I'm not sure I remember who was there. We got some nice presents, though, including the charming luncheon set from your mom and dad, you and Jackie; a large circular gilt-edged mirror from Aunt Mildred and Uncle O.B., and a watercolor done by Frank's friend, Johnny Atterbury.

We stayed overnight at the Seneca Hotel and left the next day for Elmira by train. Since Cliff was brought up in Horseheads he knew all the good places to see in Elmira. I think I was most impressed with Mark Twain's octagonal studio where he did his writing.

Working and being married is a whole other ballgame. Getting two of us up and out to the bus by 7:30 in the morning is no easy task. Then coming home, getting dinner plus any other house chores needing to be done takes more time than I ever plan. I'm sure this will get easier as I get into some kind of routine - at least I hope it will!

We went to Cliff's mother's for Thanksgiving dinner but I wasn't able to eat anything. Just before we left our place Cliff got upset about something and hit me in the jaw. It swelled up a lot but when we got to his mother's Duke, his brother-in-law, who is a doctor, took a look at it and said it was only bruised. Not too comfortable, though.

Mom and Dad are planning on having Helen, Cliff and me over for Christmas. Hope it all goes well, and the weather is not too snowy! It will be hard with the boys not there to share it with us.

Love,

Barbara

March, 1943

Dear Jean,

Lots of news from this end. First of all, Cliff lost his job at the Todd Company and has been looking for another. He is now in Jamaica, New York, trying a job down there and looking for a place for us to live. I'm back home with Mom and dad. I'm still feeling punk with - no, not morning sickness - all day sickness!! I am hoping this will go away soon before I go crazy. I don't even know how I feel about moving to Jamaica where I won't know a soul!

Mom has become a Rosie the Riveter! She has taken a factory job at Rochester Products where Frank worked before he went in service. This is the first time she has had a job since before she married my dad. I think the long bus ride, with having to transfer, is harder on her than the job itself.

My parents are still trying to accept Cliff. Of course when we wanted to get married they felt we should wait, and now that he has lost his job it doesn't do much to instill their confidence in his ability to support me. My mother has mixed feelings about the coming baby, too. She's sorry it's happening so soon but she's delighted that she will have another baby to play with and make clothes for. She really misses Barbie a lot and so do I.

I am going to Sibley's to get a couple of maternity dresses. Hopefully, I can find something that won't make me look like a house and a lot.

Cliff has three brothers that are in service, too, so with my three I have to write at least six letters every couple of weeks. And all the letters have to be cheerful! Not an easy task.

I was over visiting your mother the other day. She misses you since you've been gone, but Jackie is keeping her pretty busy. She's looking forward to spring so she can get back out in her gardens.

Love,

Barbara

September, 1943

Dear Jean,

I am fast learning what it takes to be a mother. I think Judy is quite a good baby, but it does take lots of time to do all her laundry (much!), boil the bottles and make the formula, etc., and I now have a five-room flat to take care of. We found a place at 179 Milbank Street - back in the old 19th ward. It is a very nice flat, and my piano fits neatly into the dining room.

We even have a front porch! Our first week in the new place my mom and my Aunt Bess came to do the "fall housecleaning." They made everything sparkle and sang the whole time! There is an older couple, Mary and Harold LeFevre and their teen-aged son, Dick, who live upstairs. Next door are Mary Beth and Ralph Romberg and Margaret and Win Fowler.

Cliff has a job at a company that has been awarded a war contract so I hope this one lasts. (This is his fourth job in less than a year.) It is downtown in the old Duffy Powers Building but what they are doing is all very hush-hush.

Frank sent the baby a V-mail, introducing himself to her. The only thing he said about his situation was that they had left Africa and were in Anzio. The censors left that in so it must mean his outfit is already somewhere else.

Did you read that Ingrid Bergman is living in Rochester? Her husband is a dentist connected with the U. of R. I guess she really hates it here.

Love,

Barbara

December, 1944

Dear Jean,

You may have gathered from some of my letters that this marriage of mine was not made in heaven. Cliff had wanted a divorce after Judy was born and I thought I had persuaded him that marriage is "until death do us part." I guess not. He is still wanting out and the more I argue against it the nastier he gets. He told me he actually went to the draft board recently and volunteered to go in the Army. They told him that medically they couldn't take him. After his car accident he was in a coma for several days and if he was to be sent anywhere there was extreme temperatures it could kill him. This is another case in which he feels he is personally being rejected and he can't stand that.

Jimmy is a good baby, thank goodness, and Judy thinks he is very cute. She calls him "Boo." My mom and dad love both the kids and from time to time Mom calls and says, "We'll be over to take the babies. You can go downtown shopping if you want." Do I ever!

We have just had one huge snowstorm. Everything was closed down for two days - no buses ran and all businesses and schools were closed. Thank goodness I had done some grocery shopping the day before so we had enough to eat while we were snowed in. Not fun, though.

Love,

Barbara

May, 1945

Dear Jean,

So much has been packed into these last few months I hardly know where to start. Frank wrote to Mom and Dad saying that he was going to marry Suzanne Merklen from Thaon-Les-Vosges, France, on March 17th. They planned a civil ceremony there (married by the mayor of the town) and will have a religious ceremony when they are both in the States. He described her as cute, dark hair and big, brown eyes. Mom has mixed feelings, I think. She is pleased for Frank but unsure how she will feel about a daughter-in-law who doesn't speak English. We all wrote immediately to Suzanne to welcome her into the family. Me, in halting French, Mom and Dad in English for Frank to translate.

Mom came down with a cold a couple of months ago and can't seem to shake the cough. I hope she will go to the doctor about it soon. It's not like her to be sick for any length of time at all. In fact, I don't remember her ever being sick, except for her "sick headaches," which she gets from time to time. But they are over in a day.

Wasn't it terrible about FDR dying? No matter how people thought of him politically it doesn't seem fair that he didn't live to see the end of the war. And the headlines for VE Day were as big as the headlines when war was declared. Now I hope the boys in the Pacific will be able to come home soon, also.

I am really looking forward to having a new "sister." Helen and I get along very well and I hope Suzy and I will, too. If she loves Frank she's O.K. in my book.

Love,

Barbara

September, 1945

Dear Jean,

I hate having to relate bad news, and I am no good at it, either. I don't know how to ease into it gracefully, so I will just give the facts as they happened.

Remember how my mom was always busy doing something? If she wasn't cleaning, she was washing windows, or baking or sewing or ironing. The only times I ever saw her sitting down (except for meals) was late in the evening - and even then she was reading or knitting.

So when that cough she had got worse and she had to sit down after doing just a tiny bit of work I began to really see that something serious was happening. The doctors (I think she went to two or three) didn't seem to know what was wrong, or they weren't saying. In June they put her in the hospital for tests and later said they thought she had about two years to live. In July when she became bedridden, Bill appeared (I think my dad may have gotten in touch with him) and he took over. He took care of Mom, he cleaned, he cooked, he did everything. (One day he called me on the phone and I asked him what he was doing. "Oh," he said, "I washed and starched all the downstairs curtains, then made a pot of spaghetti sauce for supper and now I'm ironing the curtains." And they were the ones with ruffles!) When Bill had to go back after his two-week leave, my Aunt Bess came to help. I felt so guilty that I couldn't be doing this, but it was impossible with the two babies.

On September 11th they took Mom into the hospital to try something new - radiation therapy. The next morning Gloria Lee, who was working at the nurse's desk on Mom's floor, called and said we should all come to the hospital. I took the kids next door, and called Cliff. When we got there who was in the room but my brother Bob and his wife, Helen! He had just arrived in Rochester the day before. Dad and Aunt Mildred were in the room, too. My mother was in an oxygen tent and breathing very poorly. Dad took me aside and said that all of his letters to Frank had been returned, which meant Frank was on his way back. Did I think we should tell Mom? I said I thought it might excite her too much. I wish we had told her.

We stayed at the hospital until Cliff and I had to go home to pick up the kids. Dad stopped at our house on his way home at 8:00 and said that Mom had looked some better and Helen was going to stay with her during the night. At 9:15 Helen called and said that Mom had passed away. This is the kind of news that doesn't seem to make sense and is impossible to accept. I think I pretty much knew, when we first saw Mom in the hospital, that she wasn't going to get better, but when the worst actually happens you can not believe it.

There were so many people that came to the funeral parlor! Terrace Park neighbors, old friends and friends of the boys. Even Clara came - remember her? She used to come and help with the heavy cleaning back when you and I were little.

The day of the funeral we got a telegram from Frank saying he was back in the States. We had never written to him about her illness (why upset him when he couldn't do anything about it?). Poor Frank - he will be devastated when he gets home.

I apologize for being the bearer of such bad news. I know you felt my mom was your second mom, as I feel the same way about yours, so this is going to be as hard for you as it is for me.

Love,

Barbara

July, 1946

Dear Jean,

Our house has become a foreign language school. Ever since Suzy came she and I spend the days holding our French-English dictionaries and pointing to objects. She is constantly amazed at something as simple as a vacuum cleaner; she is so enamored of the washing machine she has volunteered to do all the wash!

When we all went to meet her at the train station we saw a lovely girl, frightened out of her mind, standing on the train steps in her cork-soled wedgies. I made a special meal for her first American dinner: roast beef (we had to save coupons for ages to get it), mashed potatoes, green beans and cake for dessert. My dad put a slice of meat and a serving of potatoes on a plate and said, "The first plate for Sue," as we passed it around the table to her place. She looked at Frank and asked him (in French, of course) if she was supposed to share it with all of us. He translated, "This is the amount of meat (if they could get any at all) her whole family would have in a month."

It's surprising how much the kids can understand of what she says to them in French. They have picked up the language so quickly, but always answer her in English, which helps her learn, too.

Living back at 241 Terrace Park has been an experience with five adults and two children. Ironing shirts, alone, is one full day's work. Another day to iron sheets, pillowcases, my clothes and the kids' stuff. I had never paid any attention when my mom would tell me how to made a pie crust, biscuits or rolls. Now when I am in the midst of baking I can hear her voice saying, "Never roll the crust more than two times in one place. Turn the crust slightly and roll the next section." Is she here with me or is this a subliminal memory?

Bill wrote and invited us to come to visit him and his new family in Montreal. This came as a surprise to us, but Dad, Cliff and I decided to go, after Mrs. Conklin (who helps with the heavy cleaning) said she and her husband would be happy to stay with Judy and Jim. We drove up to Clayton in the Thousand Islands, stayed overnight and then drove on to Montreal. Canada is so clean and beautiful! The people there could understand my French, but I couldn't understand theirs! We met Bill's new wife, Helen, and their little girl, Joanie. We toured Montreal and loved it, especially the flower clock. Helen showed me a good place to shop and I got very nice winter coats for Judy and Jim for a very cheap price! It was a wonderful vacation.

Cliff and I are getting along a little better now. Perhaps he doesn't feel so much pressure to support us now that Dad is not charging us rent. Perhaps I feel more protected with other adults around. Anyway, may it continue to improve.

Frank and Sue check the want ads daily for vacant apartments but with all the servicemen home now space is at a premium.

Love,

Barbara

December, 1946

Dear Jean,

Thank you so much for the lovely Christmas greetings. I hope you had a great holiday. Ours was very nice. Both Frank and Sue and Bob and Helen were here for the big turkey dinner, and it went off very well.

I do miss my mom on holidays, even more than at other times, and my dad was extra quiet this year, too.

I don't like to write stories of how charming my children are (or even how awful they can be) to friends who don't have children, but I had to tell you these couple of things.

Judy, now three, has started singing popular songs. "Zippity Doo Da" is one of her favorites and if she's singing by herself it all goes along well, however, if she's singing with Cliff or me she sings in harmony! Can you believe that?

I think I might have told you that Jimmy talks very little. When I took the two kids to see Santa this year they didn't let the parents go up, so I told Judy to listen to what Jim said as he wouldn't tell us what he wanted for Christmas. When they came back down I asked Judy what he said but she said she couldn't hear it. From time to time before Christmas came I asked Jimmy again what he wanted and now he just said, "I told Santa." Christmas Eve when I was putting him to bed he said, "Santa is going to bring me a truck and a doll and a…" and he rattled off a whole list of toys. I rushed downstairs to the phone and called everyone I knew that would be giving him something for Christmas. Amazingly, they all fit into the categories he asked for except a hammer. Cliff went down cellar and made one out of wood so that wish was fulfilled. It was a panic time, but it all worked out perfectly.

O.K., no more stories.

Love,
Barbara

March, 1947

Dear Jean,

I didn't even realize it myself, but one of the things I missed since I left school and work was the opportunity to be creative. But my dad, in his own quiet way, knew that and for Christmas and my birthday gave me two night classes at the U. of R. I am taking Journalism and Modern Poetry. The classes are held on the old women's campus of the U. of R. on Anderson Street - just behind Cutler Union - remember? And guess who is teaching the Journalism course? Billy Lewis's dad! I never knew he was an editor at the Democrat and Chronicle, did you? He's a very thorough teacher and I'm getting As in his course!! The Modern Poetry course is taught by Hyam Plutzik who is a professor at the U. of R. and a poet in his own right. I am now finding out the <u>why</u> of my love for poetry in high school.

The only drawback to all of this is the more I learn and try to use what I learn the more Cliff hates it. Because he didn't graduate from high school he has little self-confidence in his learning abilities, so anything I achieve along this line takes away from him, in his mind. And when he feels diminished he lashes out - verbally and physically. (I have been living with this since three weeks after we were married but I don't dare tell anyone, so keep this under your hat, O.K.?) I will not give up my classes, though. It's made me feel like a complete person again, and I won't let that go.

I was surprised and pleased to hear that you are going with Bruce LeMessurier. Didn't his family live across the street from Pug Wells? I've heard that Bruce is really brilliant. Tell me more about this.

Love,

Barbara

October, 1948

Dear Jean,

Well, it's all over but the shouting. After six years of a very rocky marriage, Cliff and I decided to call it quits. We thought, to be fair, that each of us would take a child. (What seemed logical and reasonable at the time has turned out to be neither, but we can't go back on that decision now.) Chal, Jean Swart's sister who lives on Congress Avenue, offered to take Judy, and Cliff took Jim and they are living with Cliff's brother, Chuck, and his family. When we told my dad he was shocked and appalled, but at the same time told us he was getting married - to my Aunt Pansy (my mom's sister) - so we would have had to leave Terrace Park anyway. They were married on October 2nd but I wasn't invited to the wedding so I don't even know where it was held. We had to leave all our furniture there (no big loss) but without my knowing Cliff had run up some bills so I had to sell my piano to pay them. That I really felt badly about.

I applied for a job at Scrantom's (the book and stationery store) downtown. Luckily, they were looking for a person to take over the children's books, so I was hired at $30.00 a week. I was able to get a room at the YWCA on South Washington Street, known as Kent Hall, so I am even able to walk to work. The Y charges $14.95 a week for a shared room, with breakfast and supper six days a week, so I hope to be able to save enough soon to be able to get an apartment and take Judy back. Chal is charging $10.00 a week for Judy and Cliff will pay that.

None of my family has understood why we did this, so I am totally on my own for the first time in my life. Can't say that I am handling it well, but I'm sure it has to get easier as time goes by. I have been trying to see Judy on Sundays. I can get a bus to get there, but now Chal says Judy is having problems with the change and Chal feels I shouldn't see her for a while. Cliff's family is totally against me so I can't see Jim, either. If this is some kind of punishment I don't know what I did to deserve it. With both of the kids I'm able to find some things at Scrantom's, on sale, that I can send them - toys, books, etc., but it's not the same as being with them.

The roommate I have is a nice enough girl, but I don't have anything in common with her. She did say that her friend will be coming to live in Rochester at Christmastime and would I mind if she roomed with her. I said, no, I would want to do the same thing if I had a friend coming. So I will have another roommate sometime in December.

I still see some of the people that I met when I was taking classes at the U. of R., so that gives me a little social life. We go to a movie now and then and anything free that we can find to do! Or just go down to Bryant's Drug Store for a milkshake.

How are things going for you? Have you and Bruce set a date for your wedding yet?

Love,

Barbara

December, 1949

Dear Jean,

Every once in a while I think back to your wedding and what a beautiful bride you made! I'm so glad I was able to get off the time from work to go to the church, at least. And now you are off in Chicago. I assume Bruce has settled in at school and you are meeting new friends.

I really enjoy my new roommate. She is so much fun and tells me all kinds of stories about her boyfriend, Joe, and her family back in Clyde.

I'm sending you a picture of my "home" - Kent Hall. We live up on the top floor, but in the back of the building. The fire escape is right outside our room, which should be a consolation I guess, but it is also a hazard as the R.I.T. boys can climb up if they want!

This Christmas I am getting both Judy and Jim the record, "Rudolph the Red Nosed Reindeer." Have you heard it? It is really cute. Money is getting pretty tight as Cliff is not good about sending Judy's support money, so I have to pay her board from my paycheck. I have found a good way to eat on Sundays, though, as the Y does not serve meals that day. (Most of the people here go home for weekends, including my roommate, Joanne.) There is a small grocery store over on Plymouth Avenue where I can buy a day-old hard roll for seven cents and a piece of baloney for three cents. Then I can get a bottle of coke out of the machine at the Y for another five cents and there's my Sunday dinner for only fifteen cents! If I sleep late in the morning and eat around 1:00 it lasts me for the day.

Frank and Sue gave me a couple of bucks as an early Christmas present so I used some of it to go see the movie, "The Third Man," with Orson Welles and Joseph Cotton. It is a great movie and the zither background music is mesmerizing! Try to see it if you haven't already! I got the book "The Loved One," by Evelyn Waugh, out of the library, and really enjoyed it. It is a satire on funerals and cemeteries and very funny.

Dad called me to say that he heard from Bill's wife, Helen, that Bill had left. She is not going to tell Joanie that he walked out; she will say he died. What is the matter with this guy? He has no moral sense at all, as far as I can tell from his recent behavior. Maybe he doesn't know right from wrong, but why shouldn't he? The other two boys are responsible and dependable so why should Bill be different? I am as sorry for Helen as I was for Florence, in the same circumstance. Dad says she is going back to her home in Nova Scotia. What a shame.

Love,

Barbara

March, 1950

Dear Jean,

A few weeks ago Cliff called and said he had to talk to me. It turns out he was wanting to get married. The woman must have money as she offered to pay for the divorce. I asked what all this entailed and he said he had it all arranged for an adultery charge. I talked to my lawyer, Norman, and he told me this kind of thing is done all the time and if Cliff's friend is willing to pay, why not do it? The day of the hearing was awful. I had to get on the stand and answer all kinds of questions, the worst being, "Why are you not asking for alimony?" Finally, it was over, and I spent the rest of the day crying. Not that I wanted to be married to Cliff but I think it was because it was the end of a part of my life. Shortly after this Cliff called and said he wasn't getting married after all. Odd.

Cliff took Jimmy to live at his sister Helen's house in Irondequoit. Dad and Aunt Pansy were going to visit him one evening and they asked if I'd like to go along. Would I ever!! When we got there Helen welcomed Dad and Aunt Pansy, took their coats, asked them if they would like to sit down and have something to drink. I was still at the door taking off my coat. When I tried to talk to Jimmy she would come over and take him away. I felt like the unwanted guest.

Some good news, though. They got a television set at the Y! It is hard to see much as everyone who lives there wants to be watching it at the same time. It is an experience, to say the least. You sometimes wonder what the next new thing to be invented will be.

Love,

Barbara

November, 1950

Dear Jean,

This has been quite a time! In September I had to go into the hospital to check out a persistent pain in my right side. They did a laparoscopy and took out my appendix which I hope will solve the problem. I was out of work for a few weeks and when I went back they told me they couldn't have their employees getting sick so they fired me. Since then I have been looking for another job. I tried to get a factory job at Kodak which would have paid much better money but they said I was "overqualified." Next week I have an interview for a job in the cashier's office at Strong Memorial Hospital. It requires the use of office machines so I am hoping my comptometer training will pay off and I will get the job. Can I use you as a reference since you worked there for five years?

The national news sounds like we are getting ourselves into another military difficulty in Korea. Maybe Douglas MacArthur will be able to take care of it but I hope it won't mean sending more of our boys over there to fight.

A friend of mine who was leaving the country gave me his ukulele and I have been having so much fun with it. It is great for folk songs and popular songs like "Goodnight Irene," and "Tzena Tzena Tzena." It's nice when a bunch of us get together and everyone sings all the old songs. I remember singing a lot of these with my mom and dad.

Love,

Barbara

September, 1951

Dear Jean,

Terrible news recently. Chal (the woman who has been taking care of Judy) called me at work to tell me Fritz (her husband) had died the night before! There was no warning. They were going on vacation the next day and Fritz went in to pack while Chal did the dishes. She thought he called and when she went into the bedroom he was gone. They are Christian Scientists so there were no calling hours and she didn't want me to come to the funeral. You can't even try to console them. I know Judy was very fond of Fritz (as we all were) and this could be very difficult for her. Now more than ever I have to get her back with me.

I have just heard that there is an opening for a library assistant at R.I.T. This would be a great job for me. I have missed working with books since I left Scrantom's, and also R.I.T. is just a block away from where I live so I would save all that money I have been spending on bus fare while working at Strong. I also think the pay is better, so cross your fingers for me!

A new girl just moved in across the hall from me. She is from Connecticut and was a freshman at the U. of R. She met a young man there and started dating him - a really nice guy. Her family found out he is Jewish and told Micki if this was what she wanted they washed their hands of her. She had to leave the U. of R., of course, but she found a job and a place to live (here) so I hope it will all work out O.K. She is very pretty, a whole lot of fun, and intelligent! (Not much of that around here.) David, her friend, has started taking Micki and me to Cohen's on Joseph Avenue Sunday mornings for lox and bagels. Wonderful food! I just hope she stays here. I think we could become very good friends. Since my roommate, Joanne, left, I have been looking for someone to take her place.

What good news you had - that Bruce has been recruited by the State Department! I hope you enjoy living near Washington. I've heard there are many young people working in the government now, so you will have some good friends soon, no doubt. Let me know as soon as you get a new address.

Love,

Barbara

P.S. Judy just turned 8 last month and was really upset when her birthday present from me had to be glasses! Hard to explain economics to a kid!

July, 1952

Dear Jean,

Absolutely the greatest of news! With this new job in the R.I.T. Library, which I just <u>love</u>, I got more money than at Strong, so I could afford to get an apartment AND get Judy!! I found a 3-room apartment in an old house just a block from here. It is so great: the ceilings are 12 ft. high, there is a fireplace in the living room (for show only - but it's marble), and it's only $65 a month, everything included! Judy is now with me and we are having so much fun together. Of course, our meals are nothing to brag about (mayonnaise sandwiches and beef bouillon) - but we are together, and that is the main thing. My job is from 12:00 to 5:00 and 6:00 to 9:00. A neighbor watches Judy in the afternoon and Cindy, one of the ceramic students, sits with her at night.

My friends, Micki and David, were married in June. Unfortunately, it was on the day I moved so I had to miss the wedding but I'm sure we'll still keep in touch. I am so happy they are together.

Back to the apartment - I found some wonderful dark blue fabric with a slub - on sale - and it has made up nicely into curtains. Took me forever, however, as I had to do it all by hand. A friend was moving away so she gave me her cut-down round oak table (painted an antique white), which works great for eating (if we sit on the floor) and as a coffee table. I got a sisal rug at Sears ($12.00) and a black butterfly chair ($30) so we are all set.

Some of the older photo students at R.I.T. are renting other apartments in this house so sometimes they come over in the evenings and sit around and talk. They're all nice guys but I <u>would</u> like to meet a grown-up for a change.

Don't want to close before I ask how is that wonderful baby of yours doing? Hope she's sleeping through the night by now.

Love,

Barbara

October, 1952

Dear Jean,

I think I told you before that one of the ceramics students was sitting for me. Now the nice thing that has happened is that all the students are becoming friendly. Lili, a highly talented Belgian student that is very much in need of friends, even introduced me to the two instructors in her department. Frans Wildenhain, a very attractive, outgoing man from Germany, and Hobart Cowles, from Ohio. He is a quiet, retiring person and reminds me a lot of my dad. Frans very nicely gave me a tour of the craft school. What an exciting place and what wonderful work is coming out of there! They have four departments: ceramics, textiles, wood and metal. The students all dress in jeans and they don't take academics. They spend the days at their majors, only breaking for design classes. A very different kind of college course. The students from the other departments at R.I.T. don't quite know how to take them.

One of the photography students is leaving the city so we are having a going away party for him at my apartment. Lili said that Hobart has been depressed lately so I told her to invite him, too. The more the merrier. We're going to serve bagels with cream cheese and cold cuts and potato chips. The photo guys will bring the drinks. What fun this will be!

The weather has been so nice lately and the leaves are starting to turn, so Judy and I take long walks through the area. I don't know if you were ever in this section of Rochester but it used to be the wealthiest part in the 1800s. The houses (mansions, really) are mostly brick and have towers and gables and floor-to-ceiling windows, and some have great sweeping porches. Our street has large stone walls at either end (it's only one block long) and it used to be a gated community where the gates were locked at night. I'm sending you a photo of how our house looked back in those days.

Love,

Barbara

December, 1952

Dear Jean,

Well, to my surprise, Hobart and I have been going out. (Actually, we don't go <u>out</u> as my Judy-sitter has to get home. Therefore, after I get through at the library - at 9:00 p.m. - we go to my place and sit and talk.) I was very surprised when he asked me out because he is a very reticent guy. So since we have been going together I have found out that he was born in farm country in Ohio. He has a younger brother, Orton, who is married with two children. His father was killed when Hobie was 13 in an elevator accident, so his mother worked and raised the boys herself. (Sounds like my mother, but she never married again.) Hobie was in WWII, was wounded and in a hospital for 18 months. When he came back to the States he went to college in Macon, Georgia and got his MFA at Ohio State. He started teaching at the craft school last year. I have found all this out in less than two months and others who know him would be amazed that he talked this much!! He is very intelligent, kind and has the most gorgeous eyelashes you have ever seen! I think he might be someone I could really want to spend my life with.

Christmas is around the corner and I am sending Jimmy a small camera. For Judy I have two books on horses and a record of Leroy Anderson's "Sleigh Ride." Hobie went back home for Thanksgiving so he won't go for Christmas. Maybe we'll invite him here for dinner. Since the first Thanksgiving after Dad and Aunt Pansy married (and they had me and the boys over for dinner) none of us have been invited again to their house. Anyway, now that Dad has retired they are planning on moving to Florida year round. I have gotten a little used to not seeing him much, but I know I will miss him when he moves.

Love,

Barbara

June, 1953

Dear Jean,

I must say we have really crowded a lot into the first part of this year! Shortly after Christmas Hobie and I decided we would marry in June, after school was out. We soon rethought and figured why wait? We were married on January 16th, in the Methodist minister's parlor. Lili Hirsh stood up for me, and Hobie's brother, Orton, was Best Man. Just Judy, Dad and Aunt Pansy, Hobie's mom and sister-in-law were present. After, we came back to my place and Bob and Helen and Frank and Sue came, too. We had cake and champagne, with ginger ale for the kids. David Shuckman, one of the photo students from downstairs, took pictures, forgetting to put film into the camera! No honeymoon - maybe later in the summer.

We applied right away for Hobie to adopt Judy. It takes six months of social worker interviews and surprise visits, plus meeting with the lawyer to make it official. At least Cliff didn't object to the adoption, but signed the papers and sent them back right away.

Bob and Helen had heard about a new tract of houses going up in Chili. They couldn't quite make the down payment so they told us to go and look at them. They are ranch houses - living room, dining area, kitchen, bath and two bedrooms on the first floor. Space for two more bedrooms and a bath upstairs, if you want to expand. Also a full basement, and a large lot. It all seemed like a good deal for $10,900 so we bought one! 19 Sierra Road, Rochester 11, NY is our new address!! It is a very nice area - the school is within walking distance, and the houses are being purchased by people with young children so that is nice for Judy. She has found out that Wiz Woodworth and Sharon Worden, both of whom live behind our house on Chili Avenue, own horses, so she is in seventh heaven! Also, Dennis Smith, who lives right across from us will be in her grade, as well as Priscilla Stoss and Cheryl Fowler who live on the next street. Next door to us are the Gubbs. He is in the Marines and they are expecting their first baby in October. On the other side are the Williamses. Two boys, Steve and Dick, from Virginia's first marriage, and Suzy, who is two. I think it made Judy feel more comfortable when she found out those boys were stepchildren, too.

And how is your new daughter? What does Carol think of the new intruder? Maybe they are close enough in age so there won't be any jealousy. I never had that problem with Judy and Jim. She would just think of awful things to get into and he would follow all her commands!!

Love,

Barbara

August, 1954

Dear Jean,

I must say this first baby of ours certainly took her time in arriving. She was due June 25th and never showed up until July 15th. And only then after we had a small tornado (with hail) on the afternoon of the 14th. After she was born Hobie said the reason she was so late is because her long hair kept getting caught. (I did have to give her a haircut when she got home from the hospital.) We named her Rebecca Jean (in your honor), and will call her Becca. Another endearing trait is she sleeps only 20 minutes at a time. But we are awfully glad she is here. Judy is not quite as sure about that as we are. She thought maybe it would have been better to have gotten a pony.

I have recently read that there are 29 million TV sets in the world. You wouldn't know it around here. We seem to be the only ones on our street with a set. Wednesday nights the fights are on and the couple next door come over to watch. Art and Hobie in the living room with the set, Maxine and I in the kitchen making pizza, with pepperoni, for snacks.

The McCarthy hearings are also big on TV. It is so awful to think one man can ruin so many reputations!

We're still trying to get our lawn in shape, but we have planted many lilac bushes, and made a nice rock garden by the back door. I always wanted to have a rock garden as nice as your mom's, but this one isn't bad.

Love,

Barbara

December, 1955

Dear Jean,

Our newest baby is also our biggest, weighing in at 8 lb., 2 oz. When Jonathan decided it was time to arrive he wasted no time. Hobie and I got to the hospital at 4:00 a.m. on November 26th and Jon joined us at 4:24!

Hobie has been busy making a bedroom upstairs for Judy. He found an old barn that had collapsed and was able to buy the nice, grey wood for the new walls of the room. He is putting in a closet as well as a window seat. It's really neat looking. Judy should enjoy having a room of her own, finally. Of course, now, she considers herself a full-blown teenager (even though she's just 12) so she spends a great deal of time primping. One day Hobie came downstairs after working on her room, only to find her in the bathroom. "I don't know why we're building her a room; she's got the bathroom," he grumbled.

I have been having a great time working with the librarian, Mrs. Potter, at the school near here. I get to do displays and bulletin boards that are really fun and the librarian is so appreciative! I don't think she realizes that this is more for me than for her!

Hobie's colleague, Frans Wildenhain, won a Guggenheim Fellowship so he will be gone for this whole year. Nicholas Vergette, a British potter, has been hired to fill his place. He and his wife, a South African, are absolutely charming, talented and funny. They will be a great addition to the craft school faculty this year. I'm looking forward to seeing them a lot. And their accents I can understand!

Love,

Barbara

July, 1956

Dear Jean,

How wonderful you now have a boy! And I love the name! Remember when we were kids and I made a "Life" scrapbook? My husband's name was Dick and I had three boys: Peter, Todd and Scott. (Funny, I never named any of my own boys those names.) How are Carol and Nancy reacting to the little one?

What do you think about this new Rock and Roll music? I like the tunes - but Elvis?? Maybe I'm getting to be an old poop, 'cause I still like the Big Band sounds. Judy doesn't seem too taken with Elvis (like the girls were with Frank Sinatra), but she has lots of new records with the new sounds, of course. "Davy Crockett" is pretty popular around our house, too.

Becca is now talking like an adult. She'll probably be reading in a year or two!! Jon started to walk last month but we found he had a problem with one foot. We took him to a specialist who said he has a club foot. They put his foot and leg in a cast. Now he is walking with the cast!

I have been getting active in the R.I.T. Women's Club. I never thought of myself as a joiner but I really love working on the projects and being a part of the groups, as well as going to the teas. I actually wear a hat and gloves at those events! Mrs. Ellingson (the President of R.I.T.'s wife) is so gracious in inviting us to her house, and she always remembers everyone's name and what department their husband works in. Quite an achievement with over 100 faculty!

Remember my telling you about the first roommate I had when I lived at the Y? Well, she is now married, with two little boys, and living in Clyde. One of the perks of driving to the Ithaca Craft Fair (with pots to sell at the fair) is we get to stop in Clyde and have dinner with Joe and Joanne. Joe runs a strawberry farm (and also is the local postmaster) and Joanne makes the best strawberry shortcake! She doesn't even have to measure any of the ingredients. When I told her how impressed I was with that she said she makes them so often all summer long she'd be drummed out of the family if she ever forgot a measurement.

Love,

Barbara

September, 1958

Dear Jean,

How different is it to have, and raise, a baby in Taiwan? I hope Sandy is doing well and also the other little LeMessuriers. Is Carol going to school there? And what is it like to have servants?

I decided this summer <u>somehow</u> we would rent a cottage and have a real vacation! I found an ad in the paper describing a 3-bedroom cottage on the lake, at a weekly price we could afford. I quickly snapped it up. (We had to rent in August as Hobie teaches summer school June and July.) Shortly before we were to go to the cottage Hobie had to be hospitalized for two days to have his gums cut back. When he left the hospital the dentist told him he wouldn't be able to eat solid food for a month. I mentally added baby food to my list of things to take to the lake. We told Judy she could invite a friend to go with us so she would have some companionship, so she asked Carol Patch from our church. Two days before we were to leave Jon came down with an earache. O.K., no swimming for Jon. Despite these little drawbacks we were all excited about the vacation. The cottage was at Honeoye, in the hilly part. When we got there we found there were about 20 steps from the road down to the cottage, then another 20 steps from the cottage down to the water. The cottage itself had 3 bedrooms, but no living room, a galley kitchen and a bathroom. O.K., no problem, we could sit in the kitchen at night and read, or something. Being 5 months pregnant, and rather hefty, it was a bit of a chore to do those steps, but I persevered. We had little bonfires on the "beach," heating up the baby food with the hot dogs. The no-swimming part wasn't a problem as it was pretty chilly that week. One day, Hobie and I took the two little ones off for some sightseeing, and left the teenagers to themselves. When we returned we found they had walked into the village, bought some hair dye, and dyed their hair black! I couldn't imagine how I could explain this to Carol's mother. All in all, it was quite an experience!

I am due the first part of December so I want to get all the Christmas shopping done early. Hope the snow will hold off this year and not make things more difficult.

Love,

Barbara

July, 1959

Dear Jean,

Meg has turned out to be a delightful child - with one fault: she is a taster like her sisters. Soon the Poison Control Line will recognize my voice! Other than that she is cute as a button - and the only one in the family with dark hair.

Judy is so excited. She tried out, and got, a part in a Community Players production. No lines, but she is on stage for most of the play. They practice almost every night, which means she has to come home on a bus that takes her to the end of the line at 11:00 p.m. We take turns meeting the bus. Can't wait to see the play!

Becca was playing at a neighbor's the other evening and she fell off the top of their slide. Compound fracture of her left arm. We spent several hours in St. Mary's Emergency Department while they put on a cast. I got her some coloring books to entertain herself (normally they are banned in our house as Hobie thinks they stifle creativity). Anyway, a day or so later she came out to the kitchen and asked, "Does G-R-A-P-E-S spell grapes?" I replied yes, without thinking, then I did a double take and went into the living room. I asked her where she saw that. She pointed to a page of the coloring book. "I thought that was it," she said. "It says 'Color the grapes purple.'" Hmmmm. I asked her how long she had been able to read. "I don't know, quite a while, I think," she answered. Lucky she starts kindergarten this fall!

How are things with you and your four? We've had a good summer here, until the accident. We've had a couple of picnics over at Bob and Helen's. They have such a nice back yard! At that end of the development it overlooks a grove of trees, so it is much prettier than ours. Frank and Sue have a small back yard, but they are on a corner so they have a nice expanse of front lawn. I don't see either couple often but it's nice to know they are close.

Love,

Barbara

November, 1960

Dear Jean,

Well, we have started looking for a new house. This is a small place for four children but also Hobie has always wanted to live in the country. Plus a place with a barn so he could have his own pot shop. (One of the advantages at the craft school is he can use all their facilities to make his own pots. However, he finds when he goes to school to work the students keep asking him questions, although it is his time off, so he gets little done.) Anyway, we have started looking on the west and south sides of town. I have the feeling it is going to be hard to find what he wants for what we can afford to pay.

I don't know how I'll do in a country place. I love where we are now. Our neighbors are so great, and we all help each other out when needed. Two of our neighbors go to the same church we do (Lutheran) so the kids are in the youth group together. Also, the church has a very active adult group and I know I would miss it a lot if we move out of this area.

What do you think of the election? As a Democrat I'm pleased but Hobie is a staunch Republican so politics are never discussed at our house! However, my dad and my brother Frank are on my side so I can have discussions with them. I think it's going to be an exciting time in our country with Kennedy as President!

My Aunt Grace called me last week to tell me my Uncle Harry died. I was so sorry to hear that. He and Aunt Maud had moved to Canada so I hadn't seen them for a long time. However, he was a lot of fun and he was the one with the beautiful singing voice that I always loved to hear.

Now, how are things with all of you?

Love,

Barbara

November, 1961

Dear Jean,

We are beginning to settle down with our newest baby, David. I think Judy decided this was the last straw (how many kids is she expected to baby-sit for?). She and two girlfriends have rented an apartment on Harvard Street. I have never felt three was a good number to have as a group; one is always odd man out, but we'll see how it works out. She has been working at the bank at Bull's Head and I think she will continue on there.

Hobie came down with pneumonia while I was in the hospital with David, so besides a new baby I had a patient to take care of! I am just glad none of the kids got it.

Both Frank and Sue and Bob and Helen have moved away. Frank got a job with the Union but it meant moving to Detroit. They found a nice, brick house and Sue seems to be happy there. Bob and Helen and the two kids have moved to Florida. Bob got a job down there with a dental company as a salesman; much as he was doing here. They had gone down there when Janie was a baby but they were in Jacksonville and that didn't work out well. This time they are in Lake Worth, a suburb of West Palm Beach. I'm sure Robby and Janie will love being close to the ocean and beach.

Oops, there goes David! Have to go. Hope all is going great for you.

Love,

Barbara

April, 1962

Dear Jean,

After two years of looking for a house every Sunday, we have finally found the perfect place, in Caledonia! It is a beautiful Victorian house, with a wraparound porch, a sweeping staircase to the second floor where there are six bedrooms each with a working fireplace and a four-poster bed, which comes with the house. On the first floor there are two parlors with fireplaces; a music room, ditto; a den also with a fireplace and panelled in non-wormy chestnut; a dining room with black walnut wainscoting. The kitchen is the only room that needs renovating, but it's big. From the kitchen a back staircase leads to the maid's quarters (the kids loved that idea!). A two-story, very attractive barn is part of the deal also. A drawback might be that a railroad runs alongside of the house, but I figure we can build a fence for safety's sake. It is within our price range and the owners accepted our offer! And, even though it is on two acres, it is at the edge of town so I can walk to all the important places - like the library, the drugstore, the grocery store, and the school. I am so pleased that what we have found is something that meets all of our requirements.

Judy has been going with a young man that she seemed pretty taken with, but I think they have come to a falling out. She is now living back home again, as the apartment with the other girls didn't work out. She has a new job at Sibley's as a telephone operator and she really likes it a lot. They also seem pleased with her work, so it may be a longer lasting job than some of the others.

Even though Hobie is happy about the Caledonia house he seems very quiet, and more withdrawn than usual. I have suggested he go to a doctor but I'm not sure he will. Men never seem to want to admit there is something wrong with them.

I must say for being a non-joiner type of person I certainly have racked up a few positions! There is always P.T.A. of course, if you are a parent, but I seem to be addicted to getting elected to secretary or vice-president; I still am active in the R.I.T. Women's Club and now I have been put on the Board of the first Chili Library. This is quite a fascinating job as it entails not only having to find a residence for the library, but hiring a librarian, dealing with all the budget problems and who knows what will come up in the future? I think Hobie feels I should be at home more, but I feel these are important projects and if I can do them, I will.

Do you think Bruce will be getting another overseas assignment, or will you be Stateside for a while?

Love,

Barbara

October, 1962

Dear Jean,

These last few months have brought about many changes. I think I wrote you Hobie was not feeling well. Tests proved that he has ulcerative colitis, a potentially fatal disease. You can imagine how shocked we were! They think it started because he was overworked. The faculty at the craft school have contracts that read they are to teach three days a week. (Hobie's days are Monday, Tuesday and Wednesday; Frans - his co-worker - works Wednesday, Thursday and Friday.) However, the contract also reads "full professional time." This means, in Hobie's case, anytime there is a kiln to be fired he has to stay to watch it, whether it is his day to work or not. He also was teaching evening school on Tuesdays and Thursdays and he was responsible for those firings as well. Many days he would leave for school at 7:00 a.m. and not get home until midnight or after. "Overworked" is hardly the word.

When I found out about his illness I called the owners of the Caledonia house and explained the circumstances to them. They were very kind and allowed us to get out of our commitment to purchase the house. I had visions of us owning a house with no income!

Hobie slowly gained strength, but for a long time could do little more than just sit. Thank goodness, the craft school had sick pay!

The first part of August Judy announced that she and Jim Burns were getting married. He runs a record store across the street from Sibley's, on Clinton Avenue, and that is where they met. He is about five years older than Judy and seems to be quite a responsible person. I think he will be able to take care of her. On August 14th they were married in the Court House in Rochester. Afterward we invited Mickey, Judy's Maid of Honor and Larry, Jim's Best Man, to the house for cake and champagne. She and Jim have gotten an apartment on South Avenue in Rochester.

One Sunday after Judy's wedding I saw an ad for a farmhouse for sale on two acres in Fishers, NY (this is between Pittsford and Victor). I thought it would be a good thing for Hobie to go for a ride and take a look at it. Thought it might cheer him up a bit. So we all piled into the car and off we went. It was rather an adventure as I didn't have the slightest idea how to get there. Anyway, we looked through the house. It had two parlors, with a fireplace in the back parlor; a small den; a dining room; a kitchen with a powder room off that; a bedroom and a storeroom on the first floor. The second floor had five bedrooms, a common room and a bathroom. Previously, there had been a barn (the silo still stood) but it had burned down a few years before. There were two outbuildings: a milk house and a smokehouse. It was next to the Thruway. I had no good feelings about the place but Hobie liked it and put in an offer that was accepted(!). I guess he was sure he could go back to work soon.

Since then we have spent our weekends cleaning the place up. We build a fire in the fireplace and have the kids stay in that room, so they are at least warm, while we work. There was about 2" of mouse droppings in the cupboards (ugh!) and the upstairs floors, which were painted, were sometimes painted over cat poop (even more ugh!). The house has no insulation and the water supply comes from a spring 1/2 a mile away. I keep trying to remember Hobie says "it has potential."

Jon and Becca will be going to Victor Central School on the school bus. There are very few houses in this area and the mail is not delivered but must be picked up in the Fishers hamlet. I am not too happy at this point but at least Hobie is feeling better and has started back to work.

Sorry about all the complaining!!

Love,

Barbara

November, 1963

Dear Jean,

Guess what exciting news I have! On September 8th (same day as my son Jim's birthday) Judy and Jim had a little girl - Michelle Suzanne. They will call her Shelly. She is so cute, and she has red hair! Not sure I am pleased about being a grandmother, but this is part of life, I guess.

I am still trying to adjust to country life. Not seeing anyone but children day after day can be wearing. Hobie finally bought a second car so at least we can drive to the post office to get the mail and to Victor to do the laundry. (The spring that our water comes from has a mechanical ram that is supposed to automatically pump the water up to the house. In reality, it needs to be restarted at least once a day, if not more often, and being a mile and a half away from the house this is a real problem.) Consequently, we never have enough water to flush a toilet, let alone do a wash.

I have to admit I was pretty close to going into the closet and shutting the door when one evening at dinner Hobie offhandedly said that Shop One (the fine-quality craft shop that four teachers at the craft school had opened) was looking for a part-time salesperson. I was so excited. "I can do that," I thought, and the next morning I called the manager and told her I was interested in the job. To make a long story short, I got the job, and arranged for a woman in Fishers to come to our house to watch Meg and David. My hours are 11-3 so I am home when Becca and Jon get out of school. I will let you know how this job works out, but so far I can't wait to go to work each day!

Love,

Barbara

December, 1964

Dear Jean,

Becca and Jon are starting to make some friends in school now. Victor is a pretty closed community and it is hard for an "outsider" to break in. All of the kids' classmates have been together since kindergarten, so it takes some time to break the ice. Now Becca has Becky Foster, Lisa DeGennaro, and Cynthia Harris as good friends. Jon is teamed up with Chris Holtz, Danny Strong, and Doug DiPaola. It certainly makes it much more fun for them to go to school! Jon and Chris are also taking an art class at the Memorial Art Gallery in Rochester, and they both like it a lot.

Jim wrote that the architecture course at Ohio State was much more than he had bargained for. He dropped out and joined the Air Force. (I don't know if his dad and step-mother tried to talk him out of it or not, but I guess it's a done deal.) He will be stationed at Plattsburgh, NY, for his basic training, so - guess what? He will be with us for Christmas this year!! I am so delighted - I haven't seen him since he was twelve and then only for one day and night.

I still love my job and now that Meg is in school one of our neighbors is watching David during the day. She has a daughter Meg's age and a boy David's, so it works out well. I did find out that Hobie doesn't want me to work. When he told me about the job opening he thought I would tell one of my friends. This must be why he has been so distant this past year. Wouldn't you think he might speak up and complain earlier than this? I can understand why he feels this way. His father was killed in an accident when Hobie was 13 and his brother 9. His mother had to go to work to support them and he must have hated the situation. But that was then and this is now. I'm not going to leave my job for this reason. If I thought the kids were suffering I would leave in a minute, but I honestly think they like me being gone.

Love,

Barbara

P.S. How do you like the Beatles? I have changed my mind about Rock and Roll. These guys have so much vitality and are so much fun!

March, 1965

Dear Jean,

I got a big surprise for my birthday this year! Bob and Helen wrote that the whole family had planned a reunion. Dad and Aunt Pansy will come over from St. Petersburg, Frank and Sue will come down from Detroit, and I will come from Fishers, for a long weekend in February! They are all chipping in for my ticket. I panicked. No way was I going to fly alone to Florida!! I told Hobie I just couldn't go, even though this would be the first time in seven years we have been together. He replied that they felt they were doing something wonderful for me and I had to go. He was right, of course. (He never says much but when he does talk he has something to say that is important. Small talk is not.)

My ticket had me changing in Buffalo, so Judy said she would fly with me to Buffalo, and visit Jim's sister, Kathy, and I would go on to West Palm Beach. It turned out to be just great! The flights were smooth with no problems and the whole trip was a revelation! A completely different world down there: an ocean with a white sand beach, palm trees, and beautifully warm weather! We went to the beach, and Helen took me to lunch at La Petite Marmitte - a delightful French restaurant in a courtyard off Worth Ave. This is a long street of very expensive, beautiful shops. We saw the wealthy homes behind walls - including the Kennedys'. We even went to a dog race and I won $6! Frank and Sue looked at several condos in the area as they want to buy one when Frank retires. I am so glad I went! The plane rides there and back even turned out to be fun!

The last part of January we had a huge blackout - the whole northeast went out, and of course, no one knew why it happened, so it was a little spooky. I have been working full time now, and riding in to work with Hobie, so I was at the craft school when the power started going. We left to go home and I was a little worried about Jon.

He and Becca have been coming home after school by themselves as they are 11 and 10 now. But Becca has been going to dance classes on Tuesdays so she wasn't home that day. When we got home we found that Jon had been very resourceful. He had tried doing his homework by candlelight, but it was too scary, so he called the neighbor across the street and asked if he could come over there. I was very proud of him but Hobie decreed that those two must have a sitter after school now also. I didn't think it was necessary - when would anything like that happen again? - but I got a teen-aged girl, Jeanne Phillips, to come home with Becca and Jon. Meg and David will still go to Irene, the neighbor that had been taking them.

Jim wrote that his company is divided and one part will go to Vietnam and one part to Libya. Thank goodness, he is in the Libya part!! He will be leaving next week.

Love,

Barbara

September, 1965

Dear Jean,

We had some disturbing news the other day. Judy and Jim came out to tell us they were splitting up. I didn't realize that they were having problems, but maybe it has been going on for a while. They asked if it would be possible to leave Shelly with us, but there didn't seem to be a way to do it. Judy said she had heard of a nursery school she could put Shelly in near where they were living, so they may try that. She and Shelly will spend weekends with us when it works out.

David is having some problems being an "only child" now, with all the others in school. Consequently, I have to see everything he does. He loves to draw and paint and even tries to make those plastic model figures. Once we get them all glued together, though, he is great at painting them. Also, from a child who never talked, now he is never quiet.

You will never guess who is Mayor of Rochester now! Frank Lamb. Remember when he was in our French class? His dad was something in local politics, too, so this must come naturally.

I had to go to the funeral of my mother's oldest sister, Aunt Stell, last week.

She had lived in New Jersey so we didn't see her often. A few months ago she came to Rochester to live with her daughter, Annette. It made me realize that all of my aunts and uncles are getting to this age, which is sad.

Love,

Barbara

March, 1966

Dear Jean,

It's been kind of an up and down year so far.

On January 16th Hobie and I had our 13th wedding anniversary. We have not been getting along too smoothly for a while so I thought by making the celebration a big one we could turn over a new leaf. Hobie had lost his wedding ring so I had one of the jewelers make a duplicate of his ring for his anniversary present. I went all out for dinner: fed the kids early, made a fire in the fireplace and served dinner in front of the fire. Coq au Vin, no less! Hobie came in, sat down and asked, "Was this the kids' idea?" That kind of took the wind out of my sails.

The last weekend in January we were completely stranded by a 3-day blizzard. As payday is the last day of the month at R.I.T. we were low on groceries. I used the last of the flour to make four loaves of bread so we would at least have sandwiches. We melted snow for water to flush the toilet! The third day it let up some and Dr. Piper from down the road came up on his snowmobile. He stopped at each house to ask what groceries we needed and then drove right <u>over</u> the Thruway to get to Bob Hunt's, our little grocery store in Fishers. Judy told us later that in Rochester all the cars parked on the street were buried. She said the family next door shoveled out four cars before finding theirs!

A friend of ours who had been a student in the woodshop at the Craft School is opening his own craft shop. He asked me if I would go to the New York Gift Show to find some well-designed items for his opening. I checked with my bosses to see if that was O.K. with them and they didn't mind. So last month I flew to New York City - my first time on a jet. I was nervous about the trip but it worked out very well and I found several vendors that I think George can use and brought back tons of catalogs for him to go through.

One of the women from the R.I.T. Women's Club that I have gotten to know very well has been going to a psychiatrist and has convinced me that I might benefit from doing the same. Anyway, I checked with my doctor and he recommended one that has his office downtown. This works out quite well because I can make my appointments before I have to be to work. He is a very nice man - kind and caring, I think. Of course, he doesn't say much (I do most of the talking) but when he does it is very much to the point!

How are your kids doing back in American schools? I'll bet they're ahead of all their classmates!

Love,

Barbara

May, 1967

Dear Jean,

I was surprised when we watched the Oscars to see that "Guess Who's Coming to Dinner" won for best picture. It's about time they recognized not only the great acting but the ground-breaking premise of the film. Too bad Spencer Tracy couldn't be there for the party.

Judy has been "going with" (or whatever they call it now) Ray Kravetz for about a year. He is a very likeable, confident man. He worked with Jim at the record store and now is planning on opening his own store. Ray is Orthodox so Judy and Shelly have converted to Judaism. Judy and Ray were married at Temple Beth El on April 16th. It was a very impressive ceremony even though we didn't understand any of it. After the ceremony there was a very nice dinner for the families and afterward a reception for what seemed like hundreds of people.

My Jim has been released from the Air Force and he stayed with us for a couple of days before going back to Ohio. It was intriguing to hear his descriptions of the people and the country of Libya. He showed me a Maltese cross that he said he got "for his mom," and did I think she would like it. I managed to say yes and praised him for thinking of her, but I had a tough time with that.

I have started working with the foreign exchange student program (AFS) at Victor High School. (Oddly enough, this is the company your dad was with in Europe during World War 1. They started the program after the war.) It is so rewarding to do something that makes such a difference, both to the student and to the host family. The chapters from the different schools in the district get together from time to time during their year stay, so the kids have a chance to exchange problems and successes with their peers. And we adults have a chance to compare notes with other chapter members. So far in Victor, we are only hosting one student but the principal has promised when the senior class reaches 150 kids we can host two students.

Love,

Barbara

June, 1968

Dear Jean,

The big news here is that R.I.T. is moving the whole downtown campus to a site in Henrietta. I think the majority of the faculty is in favor of the move: it was getting pretty crowded in the four buildings that make up the school. The students aren't pleased, though. They will be going from a school that was close to stores, movie theaters and bars (!). In place of that they will have a campus that will be self-contained and I'm sure that doesn't sound too cool to them. These kids are saying they are going from R.I.T. (Rochester Institute of Technology) to South Henrietta Institute of Technology. Check those initials! Hobie and Frans were both consulted about the layout of the ceramics department so that pleased them. We have also heard that a new school will be added on the new campus: The National Institute for the Deaf. This will be a big one since R.I.T. was chosen for this honor and Lyndon Johnson and Lady Bird will be at the grand opening. Oh, yes, I forgot. All the buildings and walkways on this new campus will be of brick. So now it's Brick City. Not a term of endearment!

A big surprise the other evening. We were just ready to go out the door to an essential attendance at a church dinner when there was a knock on the door. There stood Jim on the stoop and he said, "I'm here to introduce you to my wife!" Wife! I didn't even know he was dating anyone. Her name is Jean, and she is a pretty little thing with dark hair and eyes. Very shy. There was a lot of talking and explaining (they had eloped so no one was at the ceremony), and questions. Jim is now working at a terminal where truckers are sent out on various jobs; he is in charge of scheduling their trips. They only stayed overnight and drove back to Ohio the next day. Sometimes I wish I could be more on top of things than I am. I don't do well in unexpected situations, I guess.

Are you and the kids planning on coming to Honeoye Lake this summer? Or are your mom and dad going to visit you?

Love,

Barbara

March, 1969

Dear Jean,

I got a wonderful phone call in January. Jim called to say he and Jean had a baby girl January 9th - Kimberly Michelle. (Judy was so pleased that they named the baby after her Shelly!) All is well and they are thrilled. I hope they will send pictures soon!

Judy and Ray have had a lot of problems lately. Ray's record store didn't do as well as they had hoped and he had to close it. They couldn't afford to keep up the payments on the furniture so that had to go. He hasn't been able to find another job so this is hard on all of them. Judy is trying to get a job at an answering service. (The hours would allow her to be home when Shelly gets home from school.) I don't hold out a lot of hope that the marriage will be able to last through all these difficulties - and these are only the ones I know about.

I have been working more hours lately. Betty, my boss (the manager of Shop One), has had some very serious problems. Her husband, John, has had Hodgkin's Disease for several years but has been in remission. Recently, he started having symptoms again and the outlook is grim. Betty is trying to be with him as much as she can so I am taking over many parts of her job. I feel so sorry for Betty, John and Andrea, their teen-aged daughter; I just wish there was something more I could do for them. I don't think I will have much free time for a while.

How are things at 5305? Do you think Bruce will be called on to go overseas again?

Love,

Barbara

October, 1969

Dear Jean,

I haven't heard much from Judy since she and Ray split up. I did know that she was working at the answering service in Rochester, and that she and Ray were not getting a divorce now as they couldn't afford it. We got a letter from her last week (are you sitting down? I wasn't) saying that she is pregnant. She has been going out with Bob Preston, whom she met through the answering service and he is the father. She apologized for being in this difficulty. I called her right away and asked what we could do. She said she and Bob were living together now and they plan to stay together. That was a relief, at least. Not knowing Bob, I didn't know if he would stay or flee.

My boss's husband died in September. She decided to take a 9-month leave of absence from work and go to Boston to be with her sisters. The owners hired Stan Glassman who had been the manager of a typewriter sales and repair place. Stan is also an artist and a musician so he has a good understanding of the arts. He is a sweet man, gentle, funny and friendly. I think it will work out well for all of us. I will be working full time at least until he gets the feel of the job. The sales have been up lately and I'm sure all our good customers will be very supportive.

Since the school for the deaf came to R.I.T. the teachers have been urged to learn sign language. Hobie was taking a class in it and one of the requirements was to be part of a deaf social situation. To fulfill that, one night we went to the deaf club on St. Paul Street. I saw a notice behind the bar that they had a stop action camera for sale for $75. (Jon has been saving his money to buy one of these so he and David can make animated movies.) Hobie used all of his signing skills to make the deal and we arranged to pick the camera up the next day. This not only gave Hobie many points in his class but made Jon about as happy as he ever gets. So now, on Sundays when our friends Micki and David come over with their boys, all the kids are out in back making funny movies.

Love,

Barbara

March, 1970

Dear Jean,

Oh, boy! It seems as we get older good things and bad happen on top of each other.

The really good things: Jim and Jean had a baby boy - Jim, Jr. - in February. Can't wait till they send a picture!

At work there has been a complete turnaround. Stan wasn't as happy there as we had hoped and Betty wrote Ron and Frans to say she was opening her own shop for crafts in Cambridge, with her sisters. So now, by default or whatever, I am the manager! Won't be too much different than what I have been doing, but it will mean more money (not as much as Stan was making "because he is a man," of course).

Now, the bad thing that I am having a whole lot of trouble with: Becca, our all-A student from day one, has decided to drop out of high school! Our suggestion to take English IV in summer school and graduate early was voted down. She wants out and she wants it NOW. Talking till we were blue in the face has not deterred her one bit. I had a conference with all of her teachers and they agreed she is probably bored. I had a talk with the school nurse to see if she thought Becca might be on drugs (no). I talked to the district principal and he said it was the school that was at fault, and not to worry about her. We checked on when she could take her GED and found it wouldn't be until next fall. She has taken a job at the supermarket near here, in the Deli Department. She plans to work there until her 17th birthday (in July) and then she will apply for a job at Sibley's in the new Mall which will open in September. Typically Becca, she has this all worked out, but I am still heartsick over it, and her father is in shock. Just bad news all around.

So, where is Carol planning on going to college? There seem to be a lot of colleges in your general area so maybe she can live at home while she attends. That would save quite a bit of money.

Love,

Barbara

September, 1970

Dear Jean,

Judy and Bob had a baby girl - Robbin Lee - in May. She has not a lick of hair but beautiful dimples. The kids and I went over to "meet" her after they got out of the hospital. Shelly thinks her baby sister is really cute. The end of August they moved to Minneapolis where Bob will run a halfway house for recovering ex-convicts. This makes me nervous with Shelly in a neighborhood like this, but Judy assures me it is O.K. (She is still in her savior mood, it would seem). What will be will be, I guess.

I got a phone call from my cousin/stepsister, Kathryn, in June. She said my dad was in the hospital and the doctor feels he has something wrong that can't be cured. Hobie and I talked it over and decided Jon and I would fly down to see him. I know we can only afford to do this once, so I want it to be when Dad and I can see each other and talk. We went down for a weekend - and was it hot! But my dad was so pleased to see us! I also got to talk to his doctor who said it was Dad's heart that was the problem and he didn't expect him to live long. On September 5th Kathryn called and said he had died that morning. I will be eternally grateful we got to see him before he left.

Some changes at work. Ron has moved his studio to Maine so he will not be around to settle business problems that come up. He is still doing special orders but of course, can't have the personal appointments with customers on Thursday nights as he did before. So far it doesn't seem to have made any difference in sales.

There is talk in Rochester of putting an Expressway through the center of town. This will affect us as it will mean customers will have to go into the "bad" area to get to us. We're hoping there may be an alternate route they could use, but none has surfaced yet. We may have to move, which would be a big undertaking.

Love,

Barbara

August, 1971

Dear Jean,

I am really excited about what's happening with Shop One. The owners (Ron and Frans) have decided to add 3 new partners to the corporation. This will take the burden of the everyday running of the shop off their shoulders, as well as put some extra money into the kitty. They picked Wendell Castle (a very visible furniture sculptor/artist) and Tom Markusen (a metalworker teaching at SUNY Brockport), and me! (Thank goodness, they are letting me pay my share in installments!)

The Expressway the city planned is well on its way, so our owners have been looking for a property to buy that is located in a better neighborhood. Ron and Tom finally found a workable place on Alexander Street (just across from Genesee Hospital). Those two will own the building (it is a Victorian house that was turned into apartments; the ones on the second floor are still rented, and Shop One will pay rent). Our area will be completely gutted and redone in a "New York" look. It will be very modern and up-to-date. A totally different look from the carriage house we are in now. Customers prided themselves on "finding us," and thought no one else had. Now we will have a high profile and I think everyone involved is ready for this. Sorry to run off at the mouth on this, but I can't talk about it at home; Hobie still doesn't want me to work.

Becca has been taking classes at the community college and thinks she would like to teach elementary school. I guess the principal who told me not to worry about her was right!!

After my dad died last year, Aunt Pansy came back north to live with her daughter, Kathryn and Kathryn's husband, Ned, in Geneva. I got a call from Kathryn last month to say that Aunt Pansy had died. We all went to Geneva to be there for the calling hours. She wasn't my favorite person, but Kathryn loved her so I would never say anything against her to either Kathryn or Ned. They are such lovely people!

I hope the rest of your month's stay at Honeoye worked out well. It's so nice you can get away from the heat and humidity of D.C., for even a short time.

Love,

Barbara

March, 1972

Dear Jean,

Oh dear, I have to tell you more bad news. The end of January Judy called to tell us Bob had a massive heart attack. His heart had stopped but they got it started again and took him to the hospital. Bob's mother went to help Judy so I told her she could call collect anytime she needed to. Three weeks later he died. After the funeral Bob's mother flew back to Rochester with Shelly and Robbin. Shelly came to stay with us and Daisy kept Robbin until Judy came back two weeks later. After Judy got back she found a place to live and a job and Robbin is going to a day-care center. Shelly will stay with us until at least the end of the school year in June. So far it is working out well with her here. We all love her and she seems quite happy.

At Shop One we are planning to move the shop to the new quarters in April. This means we are getting ready to have a big sale (so we don't have to move everything) and a lot of packing. The first show we plan to have, in September, will celebrate the 20th anniversary of the start of Shop One. We are borrowing items from customers who purchased work from the four original owners over the years. We will invite Jack Prip and Tage Frid to come to the opening but not let them know it will be in their honor. I imagine we can get some good publicity for this event.

Hobie and I have finally come to the conclusion that we would be better apart. Hobie will not leave the Fishers house so I am looking for a small house to buy in the Victor school district. (I don't want the kids to have to change schools.) It is too bad it has come to this, but I hope we can remain friends and the kids will feel O.K. about having two residences. I'll keep you up-to-date on the next installment.

Love,

Barbara

December, 1972

Dear Jean,

I thought I'd kill two birds with one stone and put this letter in with your Christmas card.

Well, we have made the move. Our house was finished just after Thanksgiving and we moved in the middle of a huge snowstorm! Our new address is: 6180 Deerfield Drive, Victor, NY 14564. The house is a colonial with an attached two-car garage and a small front porch. It also has a good-sized lot so I can have plenty of room for gardens.

Hobie and I let the kids decide where they wanted to live; they are old enough to make that decision. Meg and David are with me, Jon opted to stay with Hobie, and Becca went to live in Bushnell's Basin with her boyfriend, Ronny.

When I went to the bank to get a checking account, I really got upset. The man who served me asked the usual questions: name, address, social security number, where I worked, etc. Then he smiled and said, "And you want this account for your pin money?" I saw red and replied, "Yes, and for my mortgage money, and my child support money and taxes, and..." Talk about a chauvinist!

We are looking forward to Christmas here. The living room is quite large and has a nice corner for the tree. (I plan to get a balled one so I can plant it later.) Judy and her kids will come, Jon and Hobie, I hope, and Becca and Ronny. Luckily we also have a dining room!

The neighborhood is very nice. Many young families, but some with kids Meg and David's ages, too, so that works out well. The young couple that lives next door is great fun and especially welcoming to all of us.

Hope you have a wonderful Christmas!

Love,

Barbara

March, 1973

Dear Jean,

Well, I took the plunge and bought a yellow VW bug! It wasn't the most auspicious of beginnings, however. The day the dealer called to tell me the car was ready, I was home sick with a strep throat. On top of that it was raining cats and dogs. I didn't even hesitate; I said I would be there in a half hour to pick it up. I was impatient with the salesman when he wanted to tell me all the particulars of the car. I wanted to get out and drive it home. (I had left David and Meg home alone.) So, I started out of the dealership. Oh, yes, it's raining; where do I turn on the windshield wipers? I pulled into a driveway to check the owner's manual. O.K. - wipers are now working. Oh, oh - now I have to back up. Reverse - where did the salesman say reverse was? Out comes the manual again. But I did get home and I love the car! (Now that I know how to drive it.)

Jon is graduating from high school this June and he won the part of Colonel Pickering in "My Fair Lady" that the school is producing for its musical. He can't carry a tune but they felt his acting was so good they would let him "talk" the songs. He's delighted. Funny thing, both my boys are really shy and quiet but get them on stage and it's a whole new ball game. Jon and his friend Dale are planning a trip to Virginia after school is over, to check out the colleges there.

What about this Watergate? What is happening in our government that such a thing can even occur? I don't even pretend to know how this will all turn out.

My friend Micki came over the other night with her husband. She told me she had some bad news to tell me and maybe we should go upstairs. I immediately thought something had happened to Hobie or one of the kids. She assured me they were O.K., but that she had found out my psychiatrist had died. No, I said that couldn't be possible. I have an appointment with him tomorrow. That's why I came over to tell you, she explained. (She must have thought my logic was flawed.) It took quite a while before I could accept what she was saying. There is a relationship between a psychiatrist and their patient that is like no other. In order for it to work a strong bond must be formed. He had helped me all through the problem of whether or not to stay with Hobie, and after I left he helped me be strong enough to do things on my own. To lose someone like this was indeed a blow. It will take a long time to get over.

Love,

Barbara

January, 1974

Dear Jean,

As you know, I had a semi-biggy birthday this year: the big 50. Not a lot of reasons to get excited but my kids did a nifty thing for me - they gave me a surprise party. To get me out of the house so the guests could arrive, Meg and her friend, Lori Holloway, said they <u>had</u> to go to the Mall. Lori needed something vital for school that was due the next day, so off we went. David and I sort of hung out while the girls got whatever it was Lori needed. As we were getting ready to leave a couple of Moonies came up to the girls and started in on their spiel. I thought we would never get out of there, or at the very least that the girls would join the cult. Eventually they got away and we went home. I was completely taken aback to find the driveway filled with cars! Those of us born in the dead of winter don't really expect anyone to turn out to celebrate someone's birthday, but these brave souls did. It was so much fun and the kids outdid themselves, foodwise.

Are you having the same trouble we are with the gas shortage? I have been trying to keep mine topped off so I don't run out. Nothing worse than seeing those "No Gas" signs on the pumps. The whole energy crisis is worrisome. Even the Kodak tower, which has never been dark, isn't lit up these days.

Love,

Barbara

August, 1974

Dear Jean,

This is either one for Ripley's Believe It Or Not, or a Can You Top This? See what you think.

When I moved here, directly across the street from me lived a young man with his wife and little girl. A year or so later the wife left, taking the little girl with her. Since this neighborhood is mostly made up of newly marrieds or newly familied, everyone rallied around to help cheer Dick up. Without realizing that I was jumping on the band wagon, too, I introduced Judy to Dick, as he was here quite a bit and Judy came out with the kids to visit a lot.

You may, by now, have jumped ahead of me and guessed at the outcome. I didn't see it coming, but when they announced they were getting married in September, I did think, "Good. Shelly and Robbin will have a father around." Then I thought, "And they will be living right across the street." This could be a problem or it could be wonderful and I would get to see Judy and the girls more. I certainly hope it will be the latter. I think they are going to be married in Boonville, NY, wherever that is.

So, what do you think of the President resigning? About time, I think, but I surely don't know much about Gerald Ford, except he's bound to be better than Nixon.

Love,

Barbara

June, 1975

Dear Jean,

Big changes have been going on in my work life. The other owners (now only Frans, Tom and Wendell) decided that Shop One needed a new image. They wanted it to be more like a New York Gallery than a craft shop. Under those circumstances I could not stay on as manager. I have no art background and besides that, I could not agree with the new philosophy. So Becca (who had been working with me as an office assistant) and I both left. (I can't help but feel the others breathed a sigh of relief.) This was a very sad time for me as I had gotten so much pleasure from working there. Becca got a job through my next door neighbor, Paul, at Healthtronics in Fishers. I haven't found work but I'm sure something will turn up soon. I did apply at Waldenbooks for an assistant manager's job but didn't even get an interview.

Hobie called a couple of weeks ago and asked if he could come over to talk about a problem that had come up. His "problem" turned out to be an award for Outstanding Teacher of the Year at R.I.T. He did not feel that he deserved the honor, and did not want to accept it. I tried to tell him that he had been working there for 24 years and had always given much more of himself to the job than any of the others; he deserved to be an outstanding teacher because he has had many students over the years who still phone or write him when they run into trouble with their work. After an hour and a half of talking I said, "Do whatever you think you should." I had run out of arguments.

Hope you and yours will be coming to Honeoye this summer. I always look forward to seeing you. Letters are one thing, personal contact is another.

Love,

Barbara

June, 1976

Dear Jean,

Our New Year started with good news. Judy and Dick had a little girl, Brita Jean, on December 29th (her dad's birthday). All went well - Judy does seem to have easy birthings and the whole family is loving this little blonde baby. (We did have a scare about a week before Brita was born; Judy fell the whole length of the stairs, and was bruised and sore but no other problems. I, however, never got dressed and out of the house so fast when Shelly called to tell me her mom had fallen!)

Then things seemed to take another turn. I began to think about going back to Fishers. For many reasons - I had been out of work for almost a year; Hobie's health is starting to worsen, I thought perhaps it was time to go back home. I put my house up for sale and it sold fairly quickly. (To my surprise, although I had only owned it for 3 1/2 years I cleared a good amount on it.) Hobie suggested we take Meg and David and go on a real vacation to New England. We did and had a great time, except after we got to Boston poor Meg got food poisoning and was out of commission for two days. Just before we left on our trip I had an annual GYN checkup and the doctor sent me for some new thing - a mammogram. I had never heard of such a test, but I went. My doctor said the radiologist would send me a report on the results. The next day I was surprised when my doctor called me and told me to come to his office that afternoon. They had found a lump in my breast. He told me he also made an appointment with a surgeon, and this was when I started to get angry. Wasn't any of this my choice? I told both the doctor and the surgeon I was going on a week's vacation and I would call them when I got back. On returning from the trip in my mailbox was a hospital notice for hospital admission the next day. Then I really blew up! To shorten this long story, they operated and removed an inch long lump, which was benign. So that's the good news.

Meg and I moved back to Fishers last month. The money I made on the sale of my house will go toward a new kitchen and upstairs bath. I hope this will help make the house easier to live in.

I am not sure Jon and David are happy we moved back. It doesn't appear that they had to do much in the way of chores while I was gone, with the exception of helping their dad build a pole barn.

As an experiment (not intended as such) the running away from home was a failure. Time will tell if it made a difference in the long run.

Love,

Barbara

October, 1976

Dear Jean,

Thank you, again, for your wonderfully supporting phone call when Jim died, and for the contribution toward his memorial garden. After writing thanks to those who sent cards I found I was in a kind of zombie existence. I could see what needed to be done (cleaning, laundry, etc.) but couldn't get the energy to do it. Nothing seemed important enough. I finally made an appointment with Dennis, the psychologist the kids had gone to. He said, "Get a job, any job. You need to have a reason to get up and out in the morning." I went to Waldenbooks (where I had applied before) and they hired me for Christmas help. Everyone is so nice there I'm sure I will like it. The money is nothing, but that's not why I'm working.

Must close. Thanks again for everything, and especially for being my friend.

Love,

Barbara

May, 1977

Dear Jean,

We are so excited! Meg is graduating from high school this June and has been accepted at R.I.T. She will be in the Textile Department at the School for American Craftsmen (where Hobie teaches). Weaving is something she has been into since she was about five. So glad they recognized her creative ability. She may be our first college grad. Jon started at R.I.T., switched to Geneseo then to CCFL where he took all the film courses they had. Then he either lost interest or ran out of money, I don't know which. Anyway, Meg will be living at the school so that will be a new experience for her.

I am still working at Walden's. I thought they would let me go after Christmas but not so and I am enjoying it a lot. I am "in charge" of general fiction, social sciences, self-help, biography, art and antiques and poetry and drama. Being in charge means keeping the areas cleaned and stocked. We all take turns working in the back room, opening shipments, checking in the stock and getting it out on the floor. We also work the registers and, of course, help the customers. Sales have slowed down since Christmas, thank goodness. During the holidays we have 3 registers running and lines at each register. I usually work 3 days and 2 nights a week. It has been a life saver for me!

The restoration on the house is coming along well. We are putting the kitchen/dining room in the back parlor that has the fireplace. Hobie has tried his hand at woodworking and has done a beautiful job making a black walnut fireplace surround and mantle with a floor-to-ceiling attached bookcase. And now, when I do the dishes, I can look out over the back yard rather than the Thruway as was the case originally.

Hobie's mother, who had been suffering from an undiagnosed disease, died in February. We had to drive to Ohio in shifts as both Becca and Jon had to get time off from work. The funeral was held in the Baptist Church and, it being in a small town it was very well attended. Her brothers and their wives would have almost filled the church by themselves.

Hope things are going well at 5305.

Love,

Barbara

January, 1978

Dear Jean,

Hobie and I celebrated our 25th wedding anniversary this year. The kids made us a nice meal and made a framed collage of pictures of them and the grandchildren.

The big surprise was at Christmas when Hobie made me a card with a decrepit pilot flying a plane held together with Scotch tape and paper clips. The plane was headed for Florida and the wings were two airplane tickets!! We will be going in March when R.I.T. has their spring break. We'll stay at a motel but we can do things with Frank and Sue and Bob and Helen, so that should be fun.

And on the work front - my boss at Walden's was fired and it has been hard for me to accept the new guy who came to take her place. He is nice enough, and funny, but his managing practices are diametrically opposed to Mary's. Mary was out on the floor with the rest of us, but Denis is not an on-the-floor person. He directs everything from the backroom, which means that all of our work loads are almost doubled. I don't think I will last too long under these conditions. I think if I do leave I will try for a job at the school library, either the junior high school or the high school level. I'll try to stick it out until spring or summer, but if it gets too tiring I might leave earlier.

How are all the kids doing? Are you still decorating your condo at Ocean City?

Love,

Barbara

October, 1979

Dear Jean,

Sorry I didn't get to see you this summer. As I told you, this new job at the Junior High Library included a move from the second floor of the school to the first. Which, of course, meant lots of packing up of books and carting them down to the new area. And, of course, it could only be done over the summer. However, I do love this job and the new librarian is simply great!

David graduated from high school in June but wasn't allowed to be a special student (only taking art courses) at R.I.T. While he was still in high school he had taken night courses in the art department at MCC so he at least has had some advanced art training. He is presently working as a stock boy at a dress shop at the Mall. Jon is still doing stock work at Sibley's and Becca is working at Healthtronics.

Hobie's doctor finally sent him to a specialist in lung diseases. He has been feeling much worse lately. Unfortunately, the specialist confirmed the diagnosis of emphysema but also told him he has silicosis (the black lung disease miners get). In his case it was caused by the silica in the glazes he uses and the doctor said he would have to retire. Hobie's first response was that he felt sorry for his students when they find out there is this occupational hazard. I don't know how he is going to handle retiring: his work is his whole life. Financially, I think Hobie will get 6 months sick leave, New York State Disability, and then Social Security should kick in. Of course, he's only 56 so it won't be as much as if he retired at 65, but we will be able to manage, I think. Boy, we never know what's in the future for us, do we?

Love,

Barbara

March, 1980

Dear Jean,

Well, we have good news and very bad news. Good news first: Meg has been dating a woodworker who was a Rochester native but is now living and working in Florida. To cut down this story, they were married on the 9th of March. A very lovely wedding although Hobie wasn't feeling well enough to go to it. They will leave for Florida next week. Mixed feelings there! I am glad she has found someone she can be happy with but oh, so sorry she will be far away!

Hobie retired in January, but spent a lot of his time doing over the sitting room here. He opened up the ceiling to have the beams exposed and took down the wall between the sitting room and the den, to make it one large room. All that dust, plaster and sawdust was just what he needed for his lung condition!! Last month he felt really sick and the doctor put him in the hospital. Tests taken indicated he now also has lung cancer. He was sent to an oncologist who told him the cancer was inoperable but they would be able to reduce it with radiation, and maybe give him six months to live. He started the radiation right away and goes daily for six weeks.

Hobie's big show opening at R.I.T., with three other faculty members, was the week after Meg's marriage. Hobie was able to be at the opening and talk to the students and visitors but it must have taken all his reserves. It was a big success and he sold almost all the work he had in it.

We are putting our house up for sale, so now it is a big rush to get things fixed up and ready for selling. I am glad now that we put in the new kitchen and dining room. I'm sure that will be a good selling point.

As soon as we have the house ready we will start looking for a much smaller place to live. I would like to live in a village; maybe Honeoye Falls or Fairport. Imagine reducing the contents of a 16-room house to a 4-or 5-room place! Jon, of course, has been living with one of his school buddies, Dale, so moving is no problem to him. David will probably move with us, but we'll see.

Love,

Barbara

August, 1980

Dear Jean,

We moved on August 16th so this is just a short note to give you the new address: 125 Crescent Rd, Fairport, NY 14450.

This house is ideal now that David is sharing an apartment with his friends, Jim and Kevin. It is four rooms with a basement and one-car garage. It was designed by an architect as his first home. Two bedrooms, bath, living room and kitchen. Huge floor-to-ceiling windows in the living room - double windows in the other rooms. There is a 1/2 acre of beautiful woods and flowers. I love it!

Sally Roberts, who lives next door, came over to welcome us our first day with cookies. Since then Jon calls her Mrs. Good Cookie.

I think this will be a perfect place for us.

Love,

Barbara

October, 1980

Dear Jean and Bruce,

It was so sweet of you to call when Hobie died and to be so understanding. Thank you, too, for your generous donation to the Scholarship Fund.

The church service was probably very nice but I really don't remember much about it. There were so many people who came, and a good part of them came over to the house afterward. People were so nice about bringing food and goodies.

R.I.T. will have a memorial service for him later this month. We did have him cremated but haven't decided where to put the ashes. I think it's between the Thousand Islands and R.I.T.

There seems to be so much to do - going to Social Security, and the Veteran's, and the lawyer's. I had taken a leave of absence from school and I won't have to go back until January. The way it looks now I can easily be busy until then.

Thank you again for all your wonderful thoughtfulness.

Love,

Barbara

June, 1981

Dear Jean,

It has been so nice to have Meg and Rich living back up here, and playing with Anna is so much fun. Meg just told me she thinks she might be pregnant again! Sounds like she is following in my footsteps.

I have been thinking for quite a while what I would like to do with my life now that I am alone. I decided I would like to open a bookstore. I have always liked reading and working with books so I started doing some market research in Pittsford. (You probably remember that Pittsford is the wealthiest village in the area and I know it has a large library following.) In January I signed up for a course in opening your own business at St. John Fishers and I learned a great deal from that.

Last month I flew to Florida to take care of my sister-in-law, Helen. She had a bypass operation and was due to go home so I said I would come down and be <u>her</u> nurse for a change. When I arrived at West Palm Beach airport Bob met me and said Helen had had a heart attack on the way home from the hospital so she was now in a hospital in another town! Anyway, I could visit her and take care of Bob at their place. When we weren't hospital-visiting Bob and I checked out every small bookstore around - for set-up, display and any info the owner could give me.

Arriving back in Fairport I started checking ads for stores for rent. There was one in Pittsford that sounded pretty good so Judy and I went to check it out. It had been a residence on the edge of a group of 20 small shops. Jeff, the head of the complex, wants to put two stores in the house. One in the part that was the living room and kitchen and one in the part that was the bedrooms. The two shops would share a bathroom. The living room/kitchen part sounded ideal for me so I signed a lease. I plan to open in September - this will give me plenty of time to renovate the kitchen, order the stock, etc. David will be doing murals in the former kitchen which will house the children's books, art, crafts and biographies.

Now all I have to do is all the rest. Judy's husband, Dick, will make all the built-in bookshelves as well as the free-standing ones. By ordering the books early I can make sure I will have enough stock to open. I was able to buy an old cash register from Walden's as they were getting new ones in, so that was a plus. It is all working out so easily it's bound to be the right thing to do!

Wish me luck!!

Love,

Barbara

December, 1981

Dear Jean,

I'm taking a little time out from the Christmas rush (?) to write you. There is only so much you can get on a Christmas card. I did most of my Christmas shopping the first part of September as I knew I would be working all hours after Thanksgiving.

The bookstore opening, September 21st, went very well. We put ads in the papers (thank goodness David is happy to help with the artistic part of that and Jon with the text). And I sent invitations to friends who I thought might be interested. So a good many people came (over and above the family) and most of them made purchases. Wendell Castle bought a lot of craft books for his school's library and those books are not cheap!

Since then we have had a good showing each day. The majority of customers say the same thing, "It's about time we had a bookstore in Pittsford." Just what I want to hear.

Judy's oldest, Shelly, and her boyfriend, Jim, wanted to get married and we decided it would be nice to have it at my house. I checked with Father Edman (who married Meg and Rich) to see if he would be willing to do this and he agreed. We took the furniture out of the living room and set up rows of chairs from the local church. Since only about 30 people were coming it worked out well. I made two Advent wreaths which I placed in the two large windows and it made a lovely decoration. The only downer was the Best Man was in an accident the night before the wedding so they had to get a substitute. Shelly's best friend Bobbie was Maid of Honor and her dad came from Cincinnati to give her away. It seemed to me that it was very appropriate to have my first grandchild begin her new life here.

Merry Christmas and love,

Barbara

PHOTOS

1. The Green Family, 1892
   Top row: Henry Green (father), Pansy, Anabel,
   Fred
   Second row: Grace, Stella, Sarah Green
   (mother), holding Harry, Bess

2. Headstone in Tonawanda Village Cemetery:
   "Henry C. Green Died May 1, 1900
   Aged 42 years, 6 months, 4 days"

3. The Green Family, ca. 1907
   Top row: Anabel, Fred, Grace, Harry, Pansy
   Second row: Stella, Sarah Green (mother), Bess

4. Barbara Jean Matteson, August 26, 1941.
   Daughter of Bill and Florence Matteson

5. Kent Hall (YWCA) South Washington Street,
   Rochester, NY

6. On right - 12 Livingston Park, Rochester, NY

7. House that became the Reynolds Library, then
   the Red Cross Headquarters during WW II,
   later the School for American Craftsmen at
   R.I.T.

Printed in the United States
39328LVS00002B